Warren the 13th *created by* Will Staehle

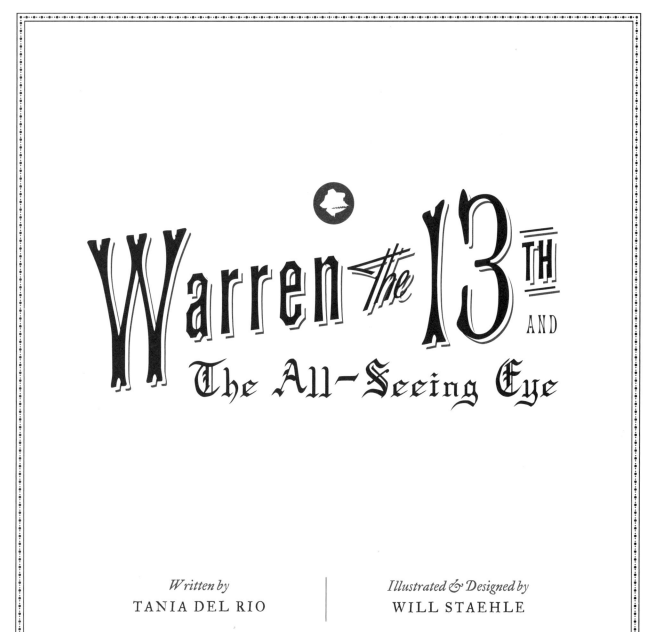

Warren the 13th
AND The All-Seeing Eye

Written by
TANIA DEL RIO

Illustrated & Designed by
WILL STAEHLE

QUIRK BOOKS  PHILADELPHIA

Copyright © 2015 by Will Staehle & Tania del Rio

All rights reserved. No part of this book may be reproduced
in any form without written permission from the publisher.

Library of Congress Cataloging in Publication Number: 2014956805

ISBN: 978-1-59474-803-5

Printed in China

Typeset in Historical Fell Type Roman

Designed by Will Staehle

Illustrations by Will Staehle

Engravings collected by Unusual Corporation and from Shutterstock.com

Production management by John J. McGurk

Warren the 13th is © and a trademark of Unusual Corporation

Quirk Books
215 Church St.
Philadelphia, PA 19106
quirkbooks.com

10 9 8 7 6 5 4 3 2 1

for our parents

TABLE of CONTENTS

ENJOY THE RIDE · RIGHT THIS WAY

CHAPTERS

WARREN *the* **13th** tiptoed across the roof of the Warren Hotel, and the old slate tiles clattered like bones. A crisp autumn wind snapped at his back, threatening to knock him off balance, but he kept going. A fall from the top of an eight-story building was the least of his worries. He had a chimney to repair.

The ravens screeched a warning from inside the smoke shaft but Warren peered down anyway. As usual, the chimney was clogged with newspapers, fabric scraps, twigs, branches, and other debris. Six black birds stared back, huddled together in a makeshift nest.

"Go on now!" Warren shouted.

The ravens didn't budge.

"There are plenty of nice trees around here. Shoo!"

But the ravens did not "shoo." They seemed to be pretending that Warren was invisible.

"I guess we'll have to do this the hard way," he said with a sigh.

Warren had performed this chore dozens of times. At least once or twice a month, he climbed up to the roof and cleared the nest from the chimney before it caused the entire hotel to fill with smoke. But this morning the ravens seemed particularly stubborn. Winter was coming, and they needed a cozy place to ride out the cold weather.

"What if I poured water on you?" Warren asked. "How would you like that?"

The birds knew he was bluffing. One snapped its beak, but the rest went right on dozing. So Warren creeped over to the ridge of the roof where a crooked weathervane stood. He unscrewed the sharp metal post and poked it inside the chimney. "I'll use force if I have to," he said with determination. "Get out of there or else!"

The ravens didn't even ruffle a feather. They knew Warren was too nice to hit a bird with a weathervane.

It was clear Warren had only one option left. "If you don't leave now," he said with as much menace as he could muster, "I'll go get Aunt Annaconda and then you'll have to deal with *her*."

The ravens exploded from the chimney, squawking and scattering feathers as they rose into the sky. They had been around the hotel long enough to know all about Annaconda, and no one—not even a raven—dared to test her patience.

Warren watched until the birds were nothing but dark specks against the dawn's pale sky. He hated to frighten them, but they'd left him no choice. His gaze lowered and he looked out from his spot high above the ground. The view was nothing special.

The Warren Hotel was the only building for miles; perched miserably on a hill in a bleak gray countryside, it was ringed by a forest of equally bleak and withered trees. You could walk for hours in every direction without finding anything interesting.

But Warren wasn't looking at the depressing view. He was looking beyond it, past the horizon, to where the rest of the world existed. He imagined cities and jungles, seaports and deserts, landscapes he knew only from books. All places he would love to visit . . . were it not for the fact that he was twelve years old and heir to his family's hotel, where he worked as the sole bellhop, handyman, exterminator, room-service valet, and all-around errand boy. Warren the 13th had spent his whole life at the hotel, just as his father and eleven other Warrens had before him.

With a sigh, he returned to the grim task of chimney cleaning. Soon his hands were black with soot. He yanked out dozens of sticks and branches and a handful of stranger, more unexpected objects: a lady's lace bonnet, a rusty nail file, a pie pan, even a bag of marbles he recognized as his own.

Warren was trying to figure out how the ravens could have retrieved a bag of marbles from the desk drawer in his attic room when a low growling noise caught his attention.

Warren squinted into the early-morning fog. To his astonishment, he saw movement in the forest. Concealed by a canopy of spindly branches, a large dark shape was weaving through the trees. The woods around the hotel teemed with bears and

wild boars, but this shape was larger than any animal. It growled again, and Warren's heart gave a leap. This was no ordinary creature.

It was an automobile!

He hadn't seen an automobile since the last guest exited the Warren Hotel, vowing never to return. Five long years had passed without a single customer. Warren's eyes grew large as the automobile crested the hill. At last, someone was coming to stay with them!

The car passed through the once-grand iron gates and slowed to a stop at the front doors of the Warren Hotel. And that's precisely when Warren remembered it was *his* job to greet new arrivals and help with their bags.

He winced as the hotel intercom sputtered to life—its tinny sound echoing inside the chimney shaft—with his uncle Rupert's panicked voice ringing through the static:

"WAAAAARREN!"

He had to get to the lobby right away! Warren considered using the chimney as a shortcut, but eight stories was a long way down. Instead, he leapt off the side of the roof, grabbed a rain gutter with one hand, and swung through a window in the attic. He landed with a thump, sprinkling soot all

over the small bed and desk that crowded his tiny room.

Warren used to sleep in one of the large bedrooms on the hotel's second floor, but Aunt Annaconda didn't like having children around and wanted him out of her way. She banished him to the hotel's topmost floor, eight floors away from the lobby where Warren did most of his work.

Dashing to a spot on the floor of his room, Warren raised a trap door, climbed down a wooden ladder, and landed with a thump inside the eighth-floor hallway. He picked himself up and ran to the main stairwell, his mind abuzz with possibilities. Who was this mystery guest? And why had this person come to his hotel?

Things had been much different when Warren was little. Back then, the hotel was booked months in advance. Grand automobiles paraded along the driveway all night long; guests arrived in style—men wearing tuxedos and top hats, ladies bedecked in gowns and jewels and pearls. A dozen bellhops in crisp matching uniforms greeted each new arrival, transferring luggage to polished brass carts while butlers swept by with trays of lemonade and cookies. In those days, the hotel had an enormous staff devoted to keeping everything in tip-top shape. Hedges were clipped, carpets were vacuumed, furniture was dusted, and wallpaper was scrubbed. A troop of maids stretched fresh linens across soft mattresses, and tall vases of fresh flowers brightened every corner.

But that was long ago, when Warren the 12th was still in charge. He died when Warren the 13th was just seven, too young to take over such a big hotel. Instead, his uncle Rupert had stepped in to fill the job. Unfortunately, Rupert was lazy and disliked work, which meant that things went downhill fast. The staff quit. The lawns became overrun with weeds. Guests cut their vacations short, then stopped coming altogether. Within a year most of the rooms were vacant, and they had remained so ever since.

Now the hotel looked more like a haunted house than a vacation destination. Once-shiny windowpanes were cracked or broken; shutters hung crookedly, and the whole building was in desperate need of paint. The interior wasn't much better. Faded wallpaper was peeling at the seams. Faucets dripped, hinges creaked, floorboards squeaked. No one had used the game room or the tearoom or any of the other common rooms in ages. The pool table was covered in dust. The furniture was shrouded beneath musty old sheets, turning tables and chairs into squat little ghosts.

"WAAAAARREEENN!"

Again Uncle Rupert's voice wailed through the intercom, jolting Warren from his daydreams. He set aside his memories and ran even faster down the winding staircase, leaping over the one-hundred-and-third step [since it was, in fact, missing] and narrowly avoiding the hotel snail lurching across the fourth-floor landing. He descended the last two flights by sliding along the bannister and then skidded,

breathless, onto the chipped checkerboard marble floor of the lobby.

Uncle Rupert stood near a window, peering through the curtains and slicking back his hair. "Th-there's a car in the driveway!" he sputtered.

Warren joined him at the window and peeked outside. A uniformed driver was unloading a small red satchel from the trunk of the car, but the passenger remained seated inside, a dark shape silhouetted against the backseat window.

"It's probably a guest," Warren said.

"But what's a *guest* doing *here*?" Rupert exclaimed. "No one comes to this hotel! Not in years! Just look at this place!"

Indeed, as with the rest of the hotel, time had taken its toll on the lobby. Sunshine seemed unable to penetrate the room; the only source of light was a tarnished chandelier that clung to the ceiling like an insect. It flickered and buzzed as if it might sputter out at any moment. Underneath sat a faded red velvet couch, its surface encrusted with a thick layer of dust—except for a large round area in the shape of Rupert's torso [he often napped there].

"It's not so bad," Warren said cheerfully. "I can dust the lobby this afternoon. Everything will look as good as new!"

Rupert stared helplessly at the wall of keys hanging behind the reception desk.

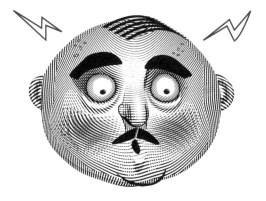

"Which bedroom is best? I've never been inside them!"

"Any of the rooms will be fine," Warren said. "I clean and vacuum them every week, just to be safe. I always knew this day would come!"

With a *whoosh*, the lobby doors swung open and a tall thin figure strode inside. The visitor was dressed all in black, except for white bandages wrapped around a strangely narrow head. Even more surprising, the guest had no luggage of any kind—only the small red satchel. Warren could hear delicate glass objects clinking inside.

Rupert gaped at the strange figure.

Warren gave a slight bow. "W-w-welcome to the Warren Hotel, sir!"

The greeting was met with silence.

"We're delighted to have you. My name is Warren. What's yours?"

The guest did not reply.

"Where are you visiting from?"

Still more silence.

"Have you come far?"

Somewhere in the distance, a cricket chirped.

The visitor reached into the folds of a long black topcoat and produced a card with a sharp *fwip!* Warren tried to accept the offering, but the guest held it just out of reach. Warren could see it was engraved with the image of a four-poster bed.

"You'd like a room with a bed!" Warren exclaimed. "Of course! We'll get you set up right away!" He looked meaningfully to Uncle Rupert, who continued to stare at the newcomer. "All I need is a room key . . . Uncle Rupert?"

Rupert finally snapped out of his trance. "Yes, yes, of course! Right away!" He turned to the rack of keys, still overwhelmed by the selection, while Warren attempted to take the stranger's luggage. "I'll be happy to carry your bag to your room. The elevator doesn't work, I'm afraid."

The guest yanked the satchel back as though Warren were diseased.

"Sorry," Warren said, shrinking away.

"Here we go!" Rupert chimed in, holding up a mottled brass key on a tattered cord. "The key to your suite. It has a lovely view! And the room number is printed directly on the surface, in case you get lost in our beautiful corridors!"

Warren eyed his uncle skeptically. It was a stretch to call any of the corridors in the hotel "beautiful," or any of the rooms a "suite," and certainly none of them had what could be considered a "lovely view." But he held his tongue as the new guest reached out a gnarled hand and snatched away the key.

Warren followed the stranger up the creaking stairway. If he couldn't carry the bag, he would at least show his new guest to the room. But the visitor whirled around and—*fwip!*—produced another card, this one bearing a large red "X."

Warren took that to mean "Leave me alone," so he gave an awkward bow and retreated to the lobby.

"I wonder if he'll expect breakfast," Warren said.

"Odd sort of fellow," Rupert muttered. "Didn't even give us a name."

Paleface, Warren decided as he imagined what might be hidden beneath all those bandages. Wounds? Scars? A third eye? An upside-down nose? Whatever it was, it had to be something pretty horrible. Why else would a person have a face wrapped in gauze?

The sound of boot heels clicking upon tile broke Warren's reverie. He turned to see his aunt Annaconda striding into the lobby. Where Uncle Rupert was short and chubby, his new wife was exactly the opposite: tall, elegant, and slender. Her long black hair was pulled tightly into a bun that resembled a viper coiled atop her head.

"Am I hearing things?" she inquired. "Or was there an automobile in the driveway?"

"My beautiful queen! My love!" Rupert exclaimed, his cheeks glowing with adoration. "You are not mistaken. We do indeed have a new guest! A wonderful fellow! He arrived just moments ago."

"Is that so?" Annaconda crooned. She scratched Rupert under his chin as though he were a cat. Rupert's face flamed fire-engine red and a purring sound escaped his fleshy lips. Warren tried not to gag. "I'm sorry to have missed him."

Warren's uncle Rupert had married his aunt Annaconda a mere four months earlier, and they still acted very much like newlyweds. They had exchanged letters for half a year before finally meeting in person. Rupert was so enchanted, he proposed almost immediately.

"Oh, darling," Rupert said, heaving a long sigh. "You are too good to me."

"No, *you're* too good to *me,*" Annaconda insisted.

"I'M THE LUCKY ONE..."

said Rupert. "Ever since you entered my life, I've felt like a new man!"

"No, I'm the lucky one," Annaconda said, throwing her arms wide and twirling. "You're my sweet handsome prince, and you brought me to this wonderful fairy-tale castle!"

Warren couldn't bear to listen to any more of their lovey-dovey talk. He tried to slink off without being noticed, but his aunt called after him. "Warren, dear, I hope you showed our esteemed guest to his room?" Annaconda smiled, causing the wrinkles around her eyes to flare like spider legs.

"He didn't want my help."

"He rejected you? Oh, my poor dear Warren, I hope you're not disappointed!" Annaconda said. "You're a peculiar-looking child, it's true, but that's no reason for adults to treat you poorly!"

She spoke so sweetly that Uncle Rupert didn't even notice the insult buried in her words. Warren ignored them. He knew he had a few strange features: a toadlike face, gray skin, crooked teeth. But he was proud of his beautiful hair—every one of his ancestors had a luxurious full-bodied head of hair—and he thought it offset the worst of his flaws.

"There's some soot in my bedroom that needs sweeping," he said. "If you'll excuse me."

"But of course, darling!" Annaconda said. "I know how much you enjoy your chores. I'd be loath to prevent you from doing them."

As Warren climbed the stairs, he could hear his uncle chuckling. "Such an odd lad. What kind of boy enjoys cleaning? He certainly didn't get that from me!"

His aunt laughed. "Of course not, my love! You're far too princely for chores."

Warren sighed. Uncle Rupert wasn't princely—he was just plain lazy. He never bothered to fix anything or clean anything or do anything that resembled labor of any kind. Warren knew that his father, Warren the 12th, would be so disappointed in Uncle Rupert. Warren the 12th always used to say that hard work built character.

Warren climbed the stairwell to the third-floor broom closet and opened the door. He sprang back in surprise. Waiting inside was Aunt Annaconda!

"Took you long enough!" she hissed, thrusting a broom into his hands.

"How did you—" Warren started to ask how his aunt had reached the third floor without passing him on the staircase but then thought better of it. She was always disappearing and reappearing unexpectedly. It was just one of her many mysterious qualities.

Annaconda stepped forward, towering over her diminutive nephew. Her gnarled hands were fixed squarely on her bony hips, which jutted out against the fabric of her dress. Gone was the smiling mask she wore in front of her husband; now her dark eyes glittered dangerously and her long face stretched into a deep snarl.

"Tell me," she hissed. "Where is this mystery guest? What's his room number?"

"I don't know," Warren said, cowering beneath her wrathful gaze. "Uncle Rupert gave him the key. I didn't see where he went."

"What did he look like? What did he say?"

"He was tall and thin . . . and he wore all black. Except for his face, which was covered with white bandages. He didn't talk, except with picture cards, and he carried a red bag."

"What about the All-Seeing Eye?" Annaconda asked. "Did he mention the All-Seeing Eye?"

"He didn't say a word," Warren said. "I think he's just a traveler passing through."

"He's here for the Eye," she whispered. "He must be! Why else would *anyone* come to this dreadful place? He's looking for the Eye, and he's planning to steal it for himself!"

Warren had heard plenty about the All-Seeing Eye, a mysterious treasure hidden inside the hotel—or so Anaconda believed. Within days of marrying Rupert, his aunt began asking about it. Warren knew the Eye was a legend, just like the giant insects that supposedly roamed the forest or the ghosts that reportedly haunted the hedge maze.

"I don't think he's here for the All-Seeing Eye," Warren said.

"You are a child and you don't know anything," Annaconda replied dismissively. "Next time you see this mystery guest, I

want you to find me right away. Do you understand?"

"I do," Warren said.

"Then close the door and leave me be."

"Leave you here? In the closet?"

"I SAID, CLOSE THE DOOR!"

Warren shut the closet door. He suspected that if he opened it again, Annaconda would be gone. But he was too scared to look.

Instead, he took the broom and climbed the stairs to the attic.

PUSH PUSH

Chapter II.

· IN WHICH ·

WARREN

PERFORMS

· HIS MANY ·

CHORES

ours later, his arms aching, Warren was still only halfway through his many chores. He had intended to sweep just his attic bedroom, but after finishing he decided to sweep the eighth floor, too. And when that was done, he couldn't help but notice the seventh floor also looked dusty. Then he decided he couldn't leave the rest of the hotel unswept. It wouldn't be fair to all the other floors!

Along the way, Warren encountered dozens of messes left behind by his aunt. Annaconda spent most of every day searching the guestrooms for the All-Seeing Eye, and her work was extremely disruptive. On the sixth floor, for example, Warren discovered a series of floorboards that had been pried up; he needed to hop up and down to wedge them into place. On the fifth floor, a carpet had been partially unraveled, so he knit the threads back together. Once repaired, the carpet didn't lay as flat as it used to [a tripping hazard!], so Warren fetched an iron and smoothed away the bumps.

In the fourth-floor hallway, Warren found a chaise with most of its stuffing yanked out—it looked like a fluffy critter had exploded. Warren gritted his teeth in frustration and set to restuffing the chair, piece by lumpy piece. But as soon as he finished that job, he noticed a hole cut into one of the walls. He didn't have time to mix fresh plaster, so instead he dragged the chair to the wall and arranged it to hide the damage. He would return later to fix it properly.

Eventually, Warren arrived at his favorite part of the hotel: the third-floor Hall of Ancestors. Hanging on the wall were portraits of the twelve previous owners—all of Warren's forefathers—arranged chronologically. Warren walked directly to the picture of his father, Warren the 12th. He looked exactly the way Warren remembered: a kind man with warm brown eyes and a long curled mustachio framing his mysterious smile.

"Father, I have exciting news!" Warren said to the painting. "The hotel has a new guest. Our first in a long time. I thought you'd want to know right away."

Warren often told his father about the latest events. He knew it was silly to talk to a painting, but he liked to pretend his father could hear him.

"He is a bit strange," Warren continued. "He doesn't say very much. And he refused to let me carry his bag to his room. But I don't care. I'm happy just to have a customer. Business is booming!"

Warren tried to keep his updates positive. He knew that his father would be saddened to learn the true state of the hotel, so he often exaggerated the good news and omitted the bad. He didn't want Warren the 12th to know how awful things really were.

"Of course, I still have a mountain of work," Warren continued. "There's so much maintenance to do before winter, so many windows to repair and heating ducts to clean. And those pesky ravens keep clogging the chimney. But I remember everything you taught me, and I won't let you down."

That was the main reason Warren worked so hard: because he knew his father had worked hard, and his father's father had worked hard, and his father's father's father had worked hard, and so on. Twelve generations of Warrens had shaped the hotel into one of the grandest destinations in the world . . . and it had taken just five years of Uncle Rupert's incompetence for everything to fall apart.

"I'll be happy when I turn eighteen and can officially take over. You're going to see big changes around here!" Warren said, smiling at the portrait of Warren the 12th.

The portrait of Warren the 12th winked back.

Or seemed to, anyway. With the afternoon sun streaming through the windows, lights and shadows bounced off the portraits in curious ways. Warren knew the wink was probably just a trick of his imagination, but he felt better nevertheless. He always felt better after visiting with his father.

Warren sat there daydreaming about happier days until the grandfather clock at the end of the hall began to chime. Soon all the clocks were clanging and gonging and bellowing, a cacophony that echoed noisily throughout the hotel.

It was four o'clock! Time to prepare dinner!

Warren hurried downstairs to the basement and ran into the kitchen. He ducked under an arc of flying carrot slices spraying from the knife of Chef Bunion and landing in a soup pot at the other end of the room. "Sorry I'm late," Warren said.

"No problem, my boy!" said Chef. "Have a seat while I finish this prep work."

Chef was the last of the family's old employees; he loved the Warren Hotel too much to leave. A burly man with thick arms, his strong hands were as big as bear paws but they moved with grace and dexterity. In fact, according to a longstanding rumor, Chef Bunion had once been a member of

the circus. One of his favorite stunts was to chop an onion, scramble an egg, and carve a turkey all at the same time. It was as if he somehow possessed four hands instead of two.

"Whatever you're cooking smells great," Warren said.

"I want you to try it," said Chef. "We'll serve you a big helping before your auntie comes sniffing around."

Warren was forbidden from eating what the rest of the family ate. Soon after marrying his uncle, Annaconda had placed Warren on a strict diet of porridge for every meal: breakfast, lunch, and dinner.

She claimed that boiled oats was the only nutrition a growing boy needed. Uncle Rupert was too love-struck to disagree, but Chef Bunion was outraged. He believed a growing boy needed vegetables and fruits, cookies and caramels. So he sneaked them to Warren whenever Annaconda wasn't hovering around.

"Tonight we have a zesty beef goulash," Chef exclaimed. "Peppers, tomatoes, eggplant, zucchini—all your favorites in a single delicious dish!" He thrust a ladle under Warren's nose.

"Mm-mmm," Warren said, savoring the smell before tasting the stew.

Chef Bunion slid a bowl across the counter and tossed Warren a hunk of bread. "Now eat up. As much as you want."

"I better leave some room for porridge, otherwise Auntie will be suspicious."

Chef Bunion just laughed. "When you've finished, chew on a mint leaf so she won't smell garlic on your breath."

Within minutes, Warren had wiped the bowl clean with his bread and was happily licking his fingers. He realized that Chef Bunion was watching him and seemed sad.

"What's wrong?" Warren asked.

"Nothing," Chef said, clearing his throat. "I was just thinking that your father used to adore this meal, too."

"He did? Really?" Warren loved learning anything about his parents, no matter how trivial the information might be.

"Oh, yes, absolutely. After your mother died, when you were just a baby, he ate it every night. It was his greatest comfort."

Warren looked down at his empty bowl and treasured the warm feeling in his belly. "No wonder I like it so much."

Chef dabbed at tears with his big pawlike hands. "Lousy onions are making my eyes water," he grumbled, turning back to the cutting board. "You better finish up and

serve dinner. You don't want to be late." And with that he tucked a treat in Warren's pocket—a pudding cookie, Chef's signature dessert of creamy chocolate mousse tucked inside a hard shell—and then sent the boy on his way.

Moments later, Warren had loaded the dumbwaiter with covered meal trays for the hotel's other occupants. First he rode up to the fourth floor and delivered a tray to Mr. Friggs, his private tutor and the establishment's only permanent guest. Mr. Friggs had been a resident for as long as Warren could remember but he never left the library, not even to venture to the dining hall. He found Mr. Friggs sitting at a desk, his face buried in a book. "Oh, is it suppertime already?" he asked, rubbing his eyes. "I do believe I've spent all day lost in this tome about the old wars of Fauntleroy. I'll have to tell you all about it in our next class. We're still meeting tomorrow morning, yes?"

"Of course!" Warren said. Meeting with Mr. Friggs was one of the highlights of his week. The old man was always quick to teach him about the extraordinary history of the hotel and all twelve of Warren's fore-fathers. He seemed to know everything about everyone.

"I heard your uncle calling for you this morning," Mr. Friggs said. "He seemed to be in a state of panic. Was everything all right?"

Warren nodded. "The hotel has a new guest!"

"A visitor! Is that so!" Mr. Friggs exclaimed. "And what is this person's name?"

Warren told him about Paleface and then explained the curious circumstances surrounding his arrival. "I'm afraid I don't have a lot of information. Not yet. But Aunt Annaconda is convinced that he's come to steal the All-Seeing Eye."

"Not that nonsense again!" said Mr. Friggs. "I have told her a thousand times: the Eye is nothing but a fairy tale. It simply does not exist!"

Mr. Friggs gestured around the library, with its thousands of journals and ledgers, its towering reams of paper. "I have the complete history of the Warren family at my disposal and I assure you, there's not a single mention of an All-Seeing Eye. There's no such thing!"

"I believe you, Mr. Friggs," Warren said. "But that won't stop Aunt Annaconda. She's convinced that it's real."

Mr. Friggs shook his head sadly. "I hate to say it, but sometimes I think the only reason she married your uncle was to get her hands on this imaginary treasure."

Lately, Warren had found himself thinking those very same thoughts. His aunt could be as sweet as a kitten when his uncle was watching. But as soon as Rupert turned his back [or fell asleep on the lobby couch], she started tearing through cabinets and ripping apart pianos. And she never even cleaned up after herself. She didn't seem to care about the hotel at all!

"Sooner or later she'll have to give up," Warren said. "She's already searched every room and hallway. There's nowhere left to look."

"I hope you are correct," Mr. Friggs said, glancing at the clock. "But right now I suspect the only thing she's searching for is her dinner. You mustn't keep her waiting!"

Warren realized he'd once again lost track of time. He hurried back to the dumbwaiter and descended to the first floor, where he placed the meals onto an old cart that, like everything else in the hotel, had seen better days. He turned and headed for the main dining hall. In the middle of the room was a large mahogany table that once sat up to twenty guests for banquet-style feasts. Warren could still remember when dinner was the highlight of every evening. All the well-dressed guests would come down from their rooms amid lively conversation and tinkling wineglasses while a live band played cheerful music in the corner. After dinner, dancing ensued and usually lasted well into the night.

But now the dining hall felt cavernous and cold. Warren pushed the squeaky cart, its wheels rattling noisily. Above his head hung the room's once-sparkling chandelier, now kept dark to save on the electric bill. Candelabras were lit instead, and their flames sent eerie shadows jittering across the walls.

Warren set a bowl of goulash and a basket of bread at each end of the table, one for his aunt and one for his uncle. Between the two he placed a tiny bowl of porridge for himself. Just as he was pouring a bottle of sarsaparilla [Rupert's favorite drink] into a glass, he heard footsteps and looked up to see his aunt and uncle entering the enormous hall. It was five o'clock on the dot, and their arrival was accompanied by the clamor of the hotel's many clocks.

With a gallant air, Rupert pulled out his wife's chair, its clawed feet scraping hard against the floor, and then scurried to take his seat all the way at the opposite end of the table. Almost immediately he began digging into his meal and making exuberant smacking noises. Flecks of tomato dotted his double chin.

Annaconda looked at her meal with displeasure. "What is this slop?" she whis-

pered menacingly to Warren so that Rupert could not overhear. "It looks unfit for a peasant!"

"It's goulash, Auntie," Warren said. "It tastes good."

Annaconda's eyes narrowed. "And how would *you* know, Warren?"

"I . . . um . . ."

"Did you try some? Without my permission?"

"My love!" Rupert cried from across the table. "Isn't this delicious? Chef Bunion has done it again! *C'est magnificentique!*"

Annaconda's frown vanished. "Yes, my dear!" she chirped back. "Chef Bunion is a treasure! But I'm afraid I have an upset stomach and I must send mine back."

"No, no! Have Warren bring your serving to me," Rupert said. "There's no need to waste a good meal."

And so Warren picked up Annaconda's plate and carried it over to his uncle, who dived in to his second helping without a moment's hesitation. As Warren returned to his aunt's end of the table, he passed by his bowl of porridge and realized it was turning cold. And cold meant gummy. Yuck.

"I'm sorry you don't like goulash," he said to Annaconda. "May I bring you something else from the kitchen?"

Annaconda leaned closer and sniffed the air around Warren's face.

"Is that garlic I smell?"

Warren quickly cupped a hand over his mouth. He'd forgotten to chew the mint! "I—I don't think so—"

"Liar!"

31

Annaconda extended a scrawny finger and flicked a speck of carrot off Warren's tie. "How did you manage to eat this slop? Has Chef Bunion disobeyed my orders?"

Warren blanched. He certainly didn't want to get Chef Bunion in trouble. Annaconda was always looking for an excuse to fire him. "N-no, Auntie. Chef didn't do anything wrong. I tried the goulash when he wasn't looking."

"Then you will have to be punished."

Warren bowed his head and waited while Annaconda tapped her chin. Thinking up new punishments was one of her favorite things to do. Like the time she sent him off to fill a sack with bear dung from the forest. Or the time she forced him to paint her fingernails and sharpen them into triangular tips. The toxic stench of her nail polish [not to mention the stinky dung!] had nearly made him puke.

"Ah-ha!" she exclaimed. "I have a good one! Your punishment is to walk the hedge maze and find its center. You'll be lost in those passageways for hours!"

The old hedge maze behind the hotel was choked with thorns and populated by wild creatures. Even during the hotel's most prosperous era the labyrinth was a scary place, and rumors soon spread that it was haunted. But that didn't keep Warren from exploring its every inch. He'd spent hours playing in the dark evergreen hedges, and he knew every turn and path like the back of his hand.

"Not the hedge maze, Auntie, please!" he begged, dropping to his knees and trying his hardest to look forlorn.

"You'll go at once!" she said, her smile widening ominously. "And there's no returning until you've found the center!"

"But how will I prove it?"

"In the middle of the maze is a statue of Warren the 1st," Anaconda said. "At the base of the statue is an inscription. I want you to copy it, word for word, and bring it back to me. Don't you dare come home until you've written it down!"

At the other end of the table, Rupert's chewing and gulping continued nonstop. Oblivious to their discussion, he had moved on to dessert, stuffing Chef's pudding cookies into his mouth at an alarming rate. Soon he would be fast asleep; he liked a good "digestive" nap after a meal.

"Now, go!" Annaconda snapped.

"Yes, Auntie," Warren said, managing to conceal his smile until he was out the door. For once, her dreadful punishment would be easy!

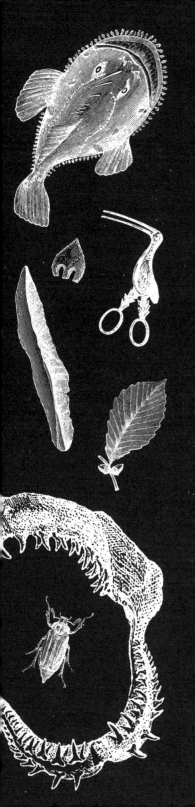

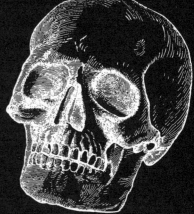

f one could see inside Annaconda's bedroom [which one rarely did, because she kept the door triple locked], one would find it quite obvious that Warren's aunt was no ordinary woman. She was a witch! Scattered about were old scrolls and books, written in strange and ancient languages. Jars of smelly oils and herbs and fish teeth cluttered every inch of the shelves. She even had a large cast-iron cauldron set squarely in the center of the room; mysterious wisps of smoke could be seen rising from within the large vessel, though it always appeared to be empty.

Annaconda retreated to this room every night after dinner. Yet again her disgusting husband Rupert had fallen asleep at the dining table; she'd left him snoring in his plate and invented some pointless errand to keep her nephew out of her hair. She needed privacy to concentrate on her new apprentice.

The robed girl sat patiently in a chair. She was twelve years old, with fair hair and skin like parchment.

"I hope your trip was pleasant?" Annaconda asked.

"Yes, Your Darkness," the girl said. "The ride was a bit long, but I'm happy to finally be here. The hotel is . . . nice."

"The hotel is horrible!" Annaconda snapped. "Absolutely miserable! A wretched place! But you will find it worth the trouble, my young pupil. I plan to teach you many skills. You'll have powers you've only dreamed of!"

The girl bowed her head. "I certainly hope that is so."

Annaconda reached into her dress pocket and pulled out a long curved object. It was the color of bone and as sharp as a claw. A dark essence seemed to emanate from it, causing her apprentice to lean forward, intrigued.

"Do you know what this is?" Annaconda asked.

"No, Your Darkness."

"This is a rare Malwoodian manticore tooth that I stole from my homeland before I was banished."

"Why were you banished?"

"The *why* is irrelevant," Annaconda snapped. "What matters is that my magical powers were stripped from me! *Robbed!* I can still transform into my spirit animal and slither across the floors—"

34

"Excuse me, did Your Darkness say 'spirit animal'?"

"Yes, yes, every evil witch has a spirit animal. We can change back and forth at will. But to do anything else, I need the tooth!"

By this point, the girl had produced a notepad and was eagerly recording Annaconda's remarks. "The tooth allows you to cast spells?"

"Only one spell remains. I'm afraid I've used up most of its magic. But when I find the All-Seeing Eye, I'm certain all my abilities will be restored. I'll be more powerful than ever!"

The girl looked up. "So why not use the tooth to find the Eye?"

Annaconda glared back. "Don't you think I've tried that?" She thrust the object toward the apprentice as if she meant to stab her. "Half these spells are failed attempts to find the Eye! You've no idea how many I've wasted in my search!"

"I'm sorry, Your Darkness," said the girl. "I will assist you in any way possible."

"Indeed, you will," Annaconda said. "You can start by shadowing my nephew Warren. Odd-looking boy. Crooked teeth and a face like a housefly. You can find him outside in the hedge maze. I imagine he'll be there all night, wandering around in circles."

"And when I find him, Your Darkness, what should I do?"

"Just keep an eye on him. I've never trusted the boy. He claims to know nothing about the All-Seeing Eye. He claims it's a fairy tale, even though his ancestors have kept the Eye hidden for twelve generations! I'm certain he's trying to throw me off the trail."

"I shall find him, Your Darkness."

And with a flash of bright light, the apprentice vanished.

Chapter III.

· IN WHICH ·

WARREN

ENTERS THE

HEDGE

MAZE

s Warren stepped inside the hedge maze, dusk was falling and the nightly fog was rolling in, casting a chilly purple haze over everything. But Warren wasn't afraid, even as hidden raccoons chittered in the bushes and crows cawed madly from the tips of the tall evergreens.

Mr. Friggs had taught Warren that the maze was more than one hundred years old, commissioned by Warren the 6th as a way to honor Warren the 1st. For many decades, a fleet of gardeners trimmed the plants and groomed the pathways and painted the signposts and cultivated all kinds of botanical surprises. But under Rupert's "care," the maze had fallen into disrepair, just like the rest of the hotel. The paths were muddy and narrow, choked with thorns. The wooden signs had faded into illegibility. Even on a sunny day, the maze remained a dark and gloomy place.

Whenever Warren ventured into the maze, he liked to pretend he was Jacques Rustyboots, the fearless explorer from his favorite adventure books; he'd call to the scuttling rodents like they were his monkeys and he'd pretend the shrieking ravens were tropical birds. He carried a stick to swish back and forth like a machete. When he passed a feral cat prowling through one of the passages, he pretended it was a tiger on the hunt. He crept around the animal carefully as it hissed at him and swatted its paws.

Eventually, Warren arrived at a tunnel that was so overgrown, he had to crawl through. He emerged in the center of the maze, where four round benches were arranged around an ancient stone fountain. A series of spigots ringed the fountain's middle platform, and weak streams of water dribbled into the basin below.

Standing on the platform was a grand statue of Warren the 1st, dressed in a military jacket studded with buttons and medals. He wore high boots and wielded a saber; underneath a furrowed brow, eyes of blank granite gazed out over the shrubbery. He looked stern and proud, a strong man, even though the statue was encrusted in a layer of bird droppings.

"Hi, Great-Great-Great-Great-Great-Great-Great-Great-Great-Grandpa!" Warren said. His eyes dropped from the statue's face to the old brass plaque mounted on the base. It was worn but still readable: "Our Brave Founder of the Warren Hotel, General Warren the 1st." Beneath that, in ornate script, was the quote Annaconda had tasked him with recording: "Those who disobey shall pay; only the righteous can pave the way."

Warren huffed. His aunt thought she was *so* clever.

He reached into his back pocket and pulled out a small sketchbook and a stub of charcoal. In the few precious moments when Warren wasn't working, he liked to draw. So far his sketchbook contained drawings of slow or stationary objects: a sleepy toad he encountered on a nature walk, the hotel snail that was always oozing around, and the ancient grandfather clock in the drawing room that told time in reverse.

Warren flipped to a blank page and prepared to write the inscription, but then he had a better idea. He tore out the paper and pressed it against the plaque. When he rubbed it with the charcoal, the engraved words appeared like magic on the page. He then had a perfect facsimile of the quote. After seeing such a fine rubbing, Annaconda would be forced to admit that Warren had successfully completed his assignment.

Satisfied, Warren lay back on one of the stone benches and looked up into the darkness. On clear nights he could see every star, but tonight the sky was hazy. He listened to the water gurgling from the fountain and let his thoughts drift, his imagination transforming the surroundings, once more, into a tropical hideaway set deep in a jungle valley.

Snap! The sound of a nearby branch breaking startled Warren, and he fell off the bench. He swore he heard the patter of running feet, but perhaps it was the sound of his own heartbeat thudding in his ears. The woods around the hotel were a dangerous place. He thought of the many bears and boars that lived there; perhaps one of the creatures had wandered into the hedge maze looking for food.

Enough dilly-dallying, Warren thought. It was time to head back to the hotel. But just as he was about to stand, he noticed something curious. Extending from the bottom of the bench was a small metal post. Warren crawled underneath and realized it wasn't a post but a latch. He tugged on it, and with a quiet *pop!* a little door opened and out fell a small book. It hit the ground before Warren could catch it, spilling several pages from its worn spine.

Warren studied the book in astonishment. Yes, the hotel was full of secret nooks and hidey-holes, but in all his years of exploring he had never discovered anything like this! On the front cover was the word "Journal" embossed in gold. He scooped up the loose pages and tucked them back in.

When he opened the book, the old leather creaked in protest. Inside the front cover was a signed book plate adorned with gears and sprockets:

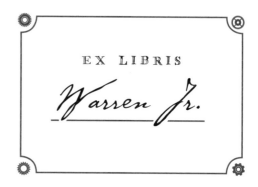

Warren gasped. He was holding the diary of

WARREN THE 2ND,

son of the hotel's founder, Warren the 1st!

He flipped eagerly to the first page and saw that the entry was dated almost three hundred years ago. The writing was scrawled in blue ink and slanted oddly to the left. At first glance, it appeared to be gibberish:

Delighted to report that plans are coming along swimmingly! Karen Jr. has managed to acquire the rest of the funds necessary to move the project forward and we anticipate that construction will begin in spring once the ground has thawed and the snow and frost clears. In the event of another war, this will certainly be the most secure

Warren turned the book upside down but the writing was still incomprehensible. That's when he realized the text was written backward! He needed a mirror, or some sort of reflective surface, to read what it said.

Just then he heard another sound—definitely footsteps this time—followed by a lilting giggle. *A girl?* Warren glanced up just in time to see a streak of white darting away.

he called out. "Who's there?"

He remembered all the old legends about ghosts haunting the hedge maze and wondered if maybe they weren't old legends after all. Again, Warren heard footsteps scurrying away, along with more laughter. He set down the fragile journal, afraid of damaging its delicate pages, and ran after the sounds.

The maze was full of confusing turns and dead ends, but Warren knew all the shortcuts. Sometimes he caught glimpses of white through the hedges, but then the figure would vanish—only to reappear moments later on the opposite side of the maze.

"Please stop running!" Warren called. "I just want to talk to you!"

He couldn't tell if it was a ghost, or a girl, or the ghost of a girl—but he hadn't seen another person his age in years and he was desperate to meet her. He ran up and down the passages, turning this way and that, until he reached the exit. But the girl was gone. Whoever [or whatever] he was chasing did not want to be found.

Crestfallen, Warren walked back to the statue to retrieve his discovery. At least he'd found something interesting to share with Mr. Friggs. He knew the old scholar would be eager to decipher the weird writing, even if it meant hours sitting in front of a mirror.

But when Warren reached the center of the maze, the journal was gone!

He let out a little cry and rushed over to the bench, looking underneath and all around. He even sloshed through the fountain. But it was hopeless. Warren was dejected—he never should have let the journal out of his sight!

A faint fluttering caught his attention and he turned to see a piece of paper trapped in a nearby hedge. Warren tugged carefully on a corner, trying not to tear it.

A single page from the journal was better than nothing.

As in the other entry, the text was written in blue ink with slanting letters. Warren carried the page over to the fountain. The water in the basin was covered with a skin of foul-smelling algae, but Warren stirred it aside until he could see his reflection. Holding the paper over the clean surface, he strained to read the words in the dimming light:

Warren gasped. *The All-Seeing Eye will appear? The All-Seeing Eye commandeered?* This could only mean one thing: the All-Seeing Eye existed after all!

When the Heart of the Warren hears
The tune played by the rightful hand:
The All-Seeing Eye will appear
Granting dominion across the land

—

And when the Heart of the Warren sees
The words writ by the rightful man:
The All-Seeing Eye commandeered,
The hotel shall no longer stand

Chapter IV.

· IN WHICH ·

WARREN

IS SENT TO

B*THE*OILER

ROOM

 s Warren entered the hotel, he was greeted by the snarl of a chainsaw. The noise was coming from Uncle Rupert. He was passed out at the front desk and snoring loudly. [Most nights he was too lazy to climb the stairs, even though his room was only one floor above.] Warren tiptoed across the tile floor. He wanted to avoid everyone until he could reach the privacy of the attic. He would use the mirror on his bedroom wall, along with his gas lamp, to examine the journal's page.

Warren creeped onto the staircase. He knew all the squeaky floorboards—and there really were quite a few—and so stepped lightly to avoid them. That required a series of complex acrobatic movements. First, he hopped nimbly from stair to stair, then did a handstand and a forward roll, and finally arrived on the second-floor landing. This was his aunt's floor. He cocked his head, listening for movement. He heard nothing but the soft tick-tock of a nearby cuckoo clock and the distant squeak of a mouse somewhere in the walls.

Satisfied it was safe, Warren exhaled and continued his ascent. When he arrived on the third-floor landing, he found an unpleasant surprise: Annaconda was waiting for him.

"Back so soon?" she asked menacingly.

"Y-yes, Auntie!" Warren stammered. Then he remembered that the hedge maze was meant to be punishment and added: "It was awful! So many strange and terrifying creatures roaming about! Please don't ever send me into that awful place again!"

Annaconda frowned. "I'm surprised. I thought you'd be wandering its passages until morning."

"I guess I got lucky," Warren said.

"Prove it," Annaconda snapped. "Give me the inscription."

Warren opened his sketchbook to show her the rubbing, and to his horror the old journal page fluttered to the floor. He reached down hastily, but with the reflexes of a viper his aunt snatched it up first.

"What are you hiding from me?" she asked. "What is this, a text written backward?"

"It's nothing!" Warren blurted. "Just a silly poem!" He waved the sketchbook in front of his aunt's nose, trying to distract her. "See? I recorded the inscription!"

"I don't care about the stupid inscription!" said Annaconda. Swatting Warren aside, she strode down the hall to a small mirror that dangled over a threadbare chair. She read the words in the reflection and shrieked with delight. Then she whirled and grabbed Warren by the shoulders. "Where did you find this? Tell me!"

"Outside," Warren said, his heart sinking fast. "It was stuck in a bush."

"Where's the next page? And the next? And the next?" Annaconda seized Warren's sketchbook and flipped through it. "Where is the rest of this book?"

"I don't know," Warren said.

"You must!" Annaconda exclaimed. "This is the proof I've been searching for! This poem mentions the All-Seeing Eye, but it doesn't say *where* it is. The other pages surely reveal more. I must have them!

Warren tried to explain how the book had vanished while his back was turned, but Annaconda insisted he was lying.

"I don't have them! Honest!" Warren cried. "If I did, I would give them to you!"

Annaconda had heard enough. She would force her nephew to tell her the truth! She reached into her pocket and pulled out the magic tooth. Warren had never seen such a hideous thing. It looked like some-

thing that belonged to a gigantic shark or a dragon. She jabbed it against his chest, its spiky tip poking through his shirt.

"This tooth has the power to make you speak," Annaconda said, pressing it even harder. Warren trembled but stood his ground, and Annaconda realized there was no persuading her stubborn little nephew. She tucked the tooth safely back in her pocket but wasn't through with him yet.

"I want those missing pages, Warren. So you better think *very* hard about where they might be."

"I can't tell you what I don't know!"

"Then perhaps a night in the boiler room will aid your memory."

The blood drained from Warren's face. Of all the punishments Annaconda had invented, this one was surely the worst. Even worse than the time she made him untangle all the knots in her hideous jewelry collection. And worse than the time she forced him to spit-shine all 203 pairs of her smelly shoes. The boiler room was the only part of the hotel that truly frightened him—a shadowy dank, claustrophobic place he avoided at all costs.

"Off we go!" Annaconda said, grabbing Warren's collar and dragging him down the stairs. She yanked open a heavy metal door with an ear-splitting *screeeeeeech,* pushed him inside, and slammed it shut. Smothered in darkness, Warren heard his aunt slide the dead bolt in place.

He banged on the door with his tiny fists. "Let me out!"

"I'll be back in the morning," Annaconda called back merrily. "Perhaps your memory will improve after a good night's sleep." And with that he heard the *click-clack* of her heels as she walked away.

"Come back!" Warren yelled. "You can't just leave me here!" He pummeled until his fists hurt and then gave the door a mighty kick, stubbing his toe. He slumped to the floor, nursing his sore foot and wincing in pain.

He was all alone.

Warren hugged his knees to his chest and lowered his head as his heart pounded with a dizzying mixture of fury and fear. He sat frozen for some time, until a deep rumbling noise made him lift his head. It was the old boiler roaring to life. Flames flickered through the metal slats, casting the room in a bright orange glow. Warren looked around.

The space was small and mostly bare except for a network of pipes that snaked along the back wall and across the ceiling, pumping heat to the rest of the hotel. On another wall hung a set of brass bells attached to cords that disappeared into the ceiling. Warren knew these were service bells from when servants lived in the basement long ago. Back then, guests would ring from their bedrooms to summon the staff. But after Warren's father installed a state-of—the—art intercom system, the bells fell into disuse.

Warren wandered over and gently flicked one. It let out a bright high-pitched *ding!* The cheerful noise made him feel a little better.

The boiler responded with a strange high-pitched whistle. It sounded like the screech of a teakettle, only slightly more musical.

"No need to be afraid, just some steam in the pipes," Warren told himself. But then the whistling was followed by a loud *bump* and a rustle and a slither.

Warren wasn't sure, but it looked like a large shadow was rising from behind the boiler. He stepped back until he was flat against the door. "It's just the shadows," he whispered. "A trick of the light."

But this trick of the light was growing wider and taller, taking clearer shape against the wall! Warren watched as two long gray tentacles reached out toward him. He squeezed his eyes shut, as if somehow that might make them disappear.

When he opened his eyes again, he saw not two but *four* tentacles groping blindly, their many suction cups quivering as they crept along the cold cement floor.

"Stop!" Warren cried as bravely as he could, but the word came out more like a croak than a command. At the sound of his voice, the monster fully emerged. Its head was large and bulbous, and it peered at Warren through a cluster of small beady eyes. More tentacles revealed themselves—now eight in all—and crept toward him with a dreadful determination. The strange beast whistled as it inched ever closer.

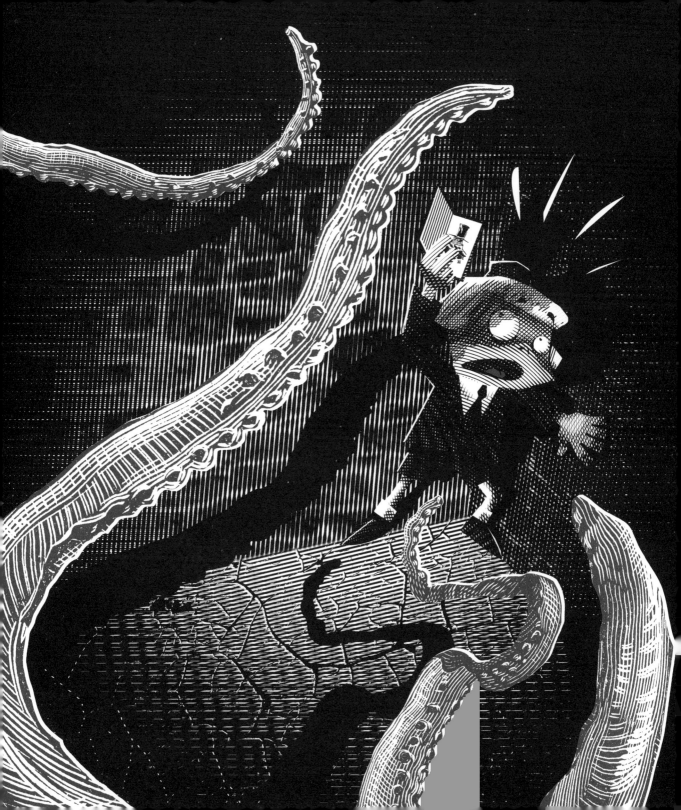

Warren sank to the floor and clamped his eyes shut. He held his sketchbook over his head—it was his only protection! He had nowhere to run, no weapons to defend himself. Nor did he have any idea what this creature was or where it came from, though he was certain he was doomed. He would be eaten, his body devoured. Rupert would never know what had happened to his nephew, and the Warren lineage would come to a tragic end.

Warren waited for the tentacles to encircle him, or for the creature's mouth to close over his head, or for some other ghastly thing to occur. Instead, he felt his sketchbook pulled gently from his hands.

Warren opened one eye. To his astonishment, the monster was holding the book in front of its many eyes, using its tentacles to flip through the pages. Warren couldn't be sure, but it sounded like the monster was whistling its appreciation!

"D-do you . . . like my book?" Warren asked.

The creature whistled louder and thrust the sketchbook toward him, wiggling excitedly. It seemed to be . . . communicating! Warren shifted to set the book aside, but a tentacle touched his wrist. Another tapped the cover. Again came the melodic whistling.

Warren couldn't imagine what it was trying to say.

"I don't understand," he said. "You want my book?"

The creature stopped whistling: *No.*

"You want a *different* book?"

That wasn't right, either—still no whistling. Warren had one more guess, but it seemed outrageous.

"Do you want me to *draw* you?"

The creature chirped happily and clapped its tentacles. Then it cocked its head and assumed a fairly ridiculous pose, like the ladies on the covers of Annaconda's fashion magazines. Warren tried not to smile as he pulled out his charcoal. "All right, then," he said. "Turn toward me. Just like that, perfect. Now hold still."

With quick thick strokes he outlined the monster and added shading and details. Just for fun, he gave the creature a top hat and a smoking pipe. When he finished, Warren signed the drawing with a small "XIII" and tore out the page. He wasn't boastful by nature, but he had to admit the likeness turned out well. "Here you go."

The creature accepted the portrait and whistled in delight. Not only that, but it seemed to be doing a little dance! Warren grinned. The creature *looked* scary, but in fact it was harmless.

"My name is Warren the 13th," he said. "Do you have a name?"

The creature whistled back and Warren realized that if it *did* have a name, it wasn't able to say it.

"I'll call you Sketchy," Warren said. "Is that all right?"

The monster clapped and trilled in approval. Then it reached out and grabbed the book and the charcoal. Sketchy stared intently at Warren, its tentacles a blur as it scribbled onto a blank page. Warren realized it was returning the favor and he tried to sit still, smiling awkwardly.

Finally, Sketchy returned the book. Warren turned it this way and that, trying to make sense of the drawing. It seemed abstract—all wiggly lines and a series of scrawls.

"It looks just like me!" he said at last, and the creature warbled cheerfully. "Wow, this is so neat! Have you always lived here?"

Sketchy nodded, whistling in affirmation. Warren was astonished. He had always avoided the boiler room—he was terrified of it—but all this time the most extraordinary playmate had been waiting there for him!

"Does my aunt know about you?" Warren asked.

Sketchy shook his bulbous head: *No way.*

"Perfect!" Warren said, grinning mischievously. "When we get out, I'll bring you upstairs and you can give her quite a scare! That'll teach her!"

Sketchy let out a chirping whistle that sounded a little like laughter.

"Is there any chance you can open this door?" Warren asked.

The creature wound several of its tentacles around the handle, tugging hard and whistling with exertion. The door creaked in protest but refused to budge. Sketchy blew out a sad little whistle.

"It's all right. You gave it a good shot," Warren said, gently patting a tentacle. "It's that stupid lock. Not to mention that the door is solid steel and probably six inches thick. We'll just have to scare my aunt in the morning, okay?"

Sketchy let out a warbling whistle and Warren smiled at his new friend. It was late and he was tired; he realized he would have no trouble falling asleep, now that he was no longer so fearful.

"If you don't mind," Warren said, "I'm going to get some rest. It's been a long day." He lay down on the cement floor and thought about the poem, repeating the words in his head so he wouldn't forget them.

Sketchy began whistling a gentle lullaby, and soon Warren drifted off. Just before his eyes closed and sleep overtook him, he was vaguely aware of Sketchy snuggling beside him, a tentacle sliding like a pillow under his head.

Chapter V.

+

· IN WHICH ·

WARREN

IS

MYSTERIOUSLY

ASSISTED

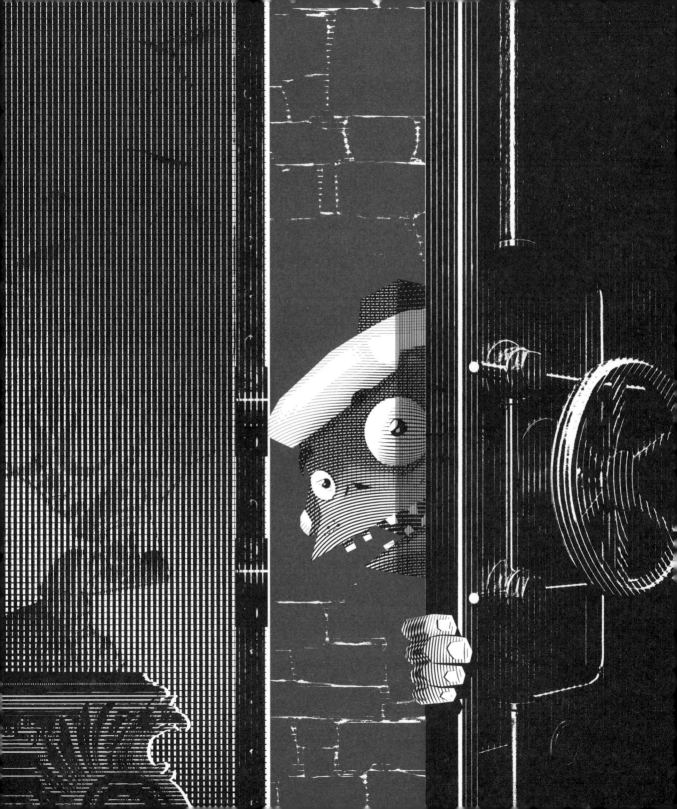

he next morning in the boiler room, Warren woke with a start. He was nestled in a coil of snake-like tentacles! But then he remembered the tentacles belonged to his new friend and he relaxed. Sketchy stirred, too, its many mini eyes plinking open one by one. Warren's stomach growled. Unless he escaped, he wasn't likely to eat breakfast anytime soon.

Fortunately, he still had Chef Bunion's pudding cookie in his pocket. Warren was hungry enough to eat the whole thing but didn't want to be rude, so he offered half to Sketchy. All the creature's eyes widened in excitement. It gobbled its portion in a single bite, then licked its lips with a slobbery purple tongue to capture every crumb.

With breakfast complete, Warren stood and stretched, his joints popping as he loosened his limbs. Likewise, Sketchy underwent a series of calisthenic tentacle-stretches, though the creature seemed to lack bones in need of popping.

Then Warren walked over to the door and rattled the handle. Still locked.

"AUNTIE ANNACONDA!"

he called, pressing his mouth to the crack of the doorframe. It was useless; he knew she couldn't hear him or didn't care. Warren had a sinking feeling. What if she never let him out? What if this was his ultimate punishment and she was leaving him there to rot away *forever*?

He sat down to think, his back against the door.

The minutes passed slowly.

Sketchy sat at Warren's side, flipping through the sketchbook and admiring the art on its pages. Warren recited the riddle from the journal, keeping it fresh in his memory: "When the Heart of the Warren hears the tone played by the rightful hand, the All-Seeing Eye will appear, granting dominion across the land."

What could it possibly mean?

What was the Heart of the Warren?

And where was the All-Seeing Eye?

Suddenly, Warren heard footsteps. He jumped up and pressed his ear against the door. He'd trained himself to recognize the menacing stomp of Annaconda—but these steps were faint.

"Hello?" he called.

From the other side of the door came a low scraping noise. The dead bolt was sliding! Sketchy let out a whistle of alarm, but Warren understood that he was being set free. He tugged on the handle and used all his strength to pull the heavy door. When he peered into the hallway, he saw a familiar flash of white disappear around a corner.

The ghost-girl from the hedge maze!

"Wait!" Warren yelled.

He turned back to Sketchy, but the creature was gone. Confused, Warren wandered all around the tiny room; he even peered into the narrow space behind the boiler. But all he saw was a sooty brick wall.

"Sketchy?" he called out. "Where are you?"

But Warren had no time to ponder his friend's strange disappearance—he needed to speak to the girl who'd set him free. He dashed out of the boiler room, rounded a corner, and spotted her at the end of the hall. "Wait!" Warren called again, but the girl slipped through another doorway. By the time Warren reached the passage, she was gone.

Just like Sketchy, she had vanished into thin air.

As Warren climbed the stairs to the first floor, he heard Rupert shuffling about, panic causing his voice to rise higher and higher. "Who's there? I need help! Somebody, *pleeease*!"

Warren quickened his pace. When he reached the lobby, he noticed something strange about his uncle. His face was red and he was sweating like he'd just been exercising [Rupert never exercised]. "Are you feeling okay?" Warren asked.

"My boy, *where* have you been? I've been in need of you all morning! I accidentally put on two left shoes and I've been walking in circles ever since!" Rupert let out a heavy sigh and plopped down onto the lobby's worn couch. "I'm so dizzy!"

Warren shook his head. Uncle Rupert had always been lazy, but he'd never seemed quite so foolish. Not until he fell head over heels for Aunt Annaconda. Now he was the most addle-brained person Warren had ever met.

Still, he tried to be kind. "Here, let me help you," Warren said, kneeling and prying the shoes off his uncle's feet. He tried to ignore the terrible odor. They smelled like warm ham.

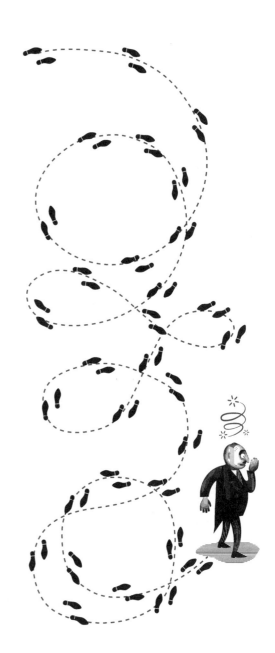

"Ahhh, that's better," Rupert said, ruffling his nephew's hair as if he were a dog.

"Glad I could help," Warren said, smoothing his curls.

"Say, we missed you at breakfast!" Rupert grinned and nudged Warren in the ribs. "Overslept, did you?"

"NOT EXACTLY,"

Warren said. He knew from experience that whenever he tried to tell his uncle about his wife's mistreatment, Rupert grew cross and never believed him. This time was serious, however, and Warren decided to tell the truth. He took a deep breath and said in a rush: "Aunt Annaconda locked me in the boiler room all night as punishment for this diary page I found that was written by Warren the 2nd and mentions the All-Seeing Eye that she's searching for but if she finds it then the hotel will no longer stand!"

"What on earth are you babbling about?" Rupert said.

"We can't let her find the other pages!" Warren cried. "She'll ruin the hotel! It's all spelled out in Warren the 2nd's journal!"

"For heaven's sake!" Rupert said, throwing up his hands in frustration.

"Don't say such horrible things about your delicate aunt! That lovely woman has a heart of gold! She's been like a mother to you! And this is how you repay her? With these terrible accusations? I know you have an active imagination, Warren, but this is ridiculous!"

"I'm not lying!" Warren said.

"Well, then, you're exaggerating." Rupert was so agitated, his face fairly glowed. "The next time you see your aunt, I want you to apologize for thinking such mean thoughts!"

Warren sighed and shuffled out of the lobby. Uncle Rupert was never going to believe him. But Warren knew of one person who would.

Chapter VI.

· IN WHICH ·

WARREN

CONFERS WITH

MR. FRIGGS

 nce in the library, Warren found his elderly teacher seated at an oak desk, surrounded by towering stacks of old notepads, binders, and leather-bound volumes. Over the years, Mr. Friggs had taken the liberty of decorating the library as though it were his own lodgings. Hanging on the walls were the many items he'd collected during his life as an adventurer: punch bowls made from giant coconut shells, macramé beaded wall art, and stone and wood carvings of animal deities. It made the room look much more festive than your average hotel library.

Warren loved asking Mr. Friggs about his long-ago adventures—like the time he went fishing with a seaside tribe on the tiny tropical island of Barrakas, or the time he hunted yetis in the snow-capped mountains

of Frostbjorn. In antique daguerreotypes, Mr. Friggs looked hale and hearty, with a ruddy complexion, well-muscled legs, and a strapping mustache. Now, Mr. Friggs was old, pale, and frail; his once-impressive mustache was no more [though he did have a striking set of muttonchops] and his false teeth had a tendency to fall out at inopportune moments. But his agile mind was as sharp as ever.

"Hello, my dear boy! Have a seat! I wasn't expecting you this early. Let me put on some tea." Mr. Friggs used his cane to shuffle to a camp stove on a nearby table. Warren looked around, but there really wasn't anyplace to sit amid all the clutter, so he leaned somewhat awkwardly on the side of a globe.

"I know I'm early for my lesson," Warren said. "But I really need to talk. You know more about the hotel's history than anyone, so I hope you can help."

"Well, goodness knows I've been here a long time," Mr. Friggs said with a chuckle, setting the kettle on the stovetop. "What do you need?"

"It's about the All-Seeing Eye," Warren said.

"Not that again!" said Mr. Friggs, giving Warren a critical look. "I told you yesterday that story is a myth. There's no such thing, and your aunt, I'm sorry to say, is a raving lunatic."

"That's not true!" Warren said. "I mean, Aunt Annaconda *is* a raving lunatic, but the Eye *isn't* a myth. It's real. I found proof!"

Mr. Friggs turned to Warren and raised a bushy eyebrow. "Oh? Do tell."

So Warren described how he had discovered—and then lost—the journal in the hedge maze, explaining how Annaconda was now in possession of the page with the poem. By the time his story was told, Mr. Friggs's dentures had fallen out in shock. He popped them back in and said, "Tell me the poem again. Slowly and clearly, so my old ears can hear it properly."

Warren obliged:

"When the Heart of
the Warren hears
The tone played by the rightful hand,
The All-Seeing Eye will appear
Granting dominion across the land

———

And when the Heart
of the Warren sees
The words writ by the
rightful man:
The All-Seeing Eye commandeered,
The hotel shall no longer stand"

"The hotel shall no longer stand?" said Mr. Friggs. "I don't like the sound of that! It seems like this Eye could topple the entire building!"

"That's what I was thinking," Warren said.

"Are you sure the journal was authentic?"

"It *looked* real. And it was old. In fact, it was dated the year the hotel was founded."

"Well, I suppose that would make sense," Mr. Friggs said. "Warren the 1st may have founded the hotel, but it was his son, Warren Jr., who built it. He was a gifted architect and inventor—far ahead of his time."

Mr. Friggs began stroking his sideburns, a natural habit whenever he was engaged in serious thought. "I admit I've always had my doubts . . . but if anyone knew about a treasure hidden in the hotel, it would be Warren the 2nd. Particularly if he had a hand in hiding it."

"So if Aunt Annaconda finds the All-Seeing Eye, she'll get dominion across the land?" asked Warren. It was bad enough she already had dominion over Uncle Rupert and the whole hotel!

"I'm afraid it appears that way," Mr. Friggs said. "My boy, you *cannot* allow your aunt to find the Eye. You must find it first and prevent her from taking control of it. The hotel's fate rests on your shoulders! I will aid you any way I can, but I'm an old man and my adventuring days are far behind me."

Something stirred in Warren's heart. Something that felt a lot like fear, except it was mixed with something else. Excitement. Determination!

"But *how* do I stop her?" Warren asked. "I've looked *everywhere* for the Eye. So has Annaconda. She's turned the hotel inside out!"

"I wish I could tell you," Mr. Friggs said. "Annaconda may have the journal page, but you were smart to memorize the poem. Study the words. Think about what clues they may hold. And I shall do the same."

"Okay," Warren said, clenching his fists. "I'll do my best."

"And be careful. I've never trusted Annaconda, and I have a distinct feeling she may be extremely dangerous."

"You got that right!" Warren exclaimed. "Yesterday she nearly stabbed me with a giant fang!"

Mr. Friggs paled. "What kind of fang?"

"It was big and sharp, with a bunch of weird symbols carved on it. She said it was a tooth that would force me to talk."

"It can't be!" With sudden urgency, Mr. Friggs leapt from his chair. Like a dog digging for a bone, he began burrowing through piles of books. After a few moments of searching frantically, he stood holding a black leather-bound book titled *A Compleat History of Witchcraft, Good and Ill*. As he flipped through the pages, Warren stood on tiptoe to get a better look. Eventually, Mr. Friggs landed on an engraving of a tooth—a tooth that looked eerily similar to Aunt Annaconda's.

"That's it!" Warren cried.

"Then things are worse than I feared," Mr. Friggs said, his voice a hoarse whisper. "This is a Malwoodian manticore scrimshaw tooth! The manticore went extinct thousands of years ago; their teeth are extremely rare. It's said that only the most powerful witches possess them."

"Witches?" Warren repeated.

"They're used for spells. Curses and dark magic." Mr. Friggs said, shaking his head in dismay. "I hate to say it, my boy, but our situation is far more dire than we thought!"

ANTICORE

nnaconda paced anxiously in her chamber, clutching the page she'd seized from Warren and trying her best to make sense of the poem. Her fists clamped the paper so tightly it was now as limp as a tissue; even the ink had begun to run. Annaconda worried that the words would be illegible before she had a chance to decode them, and yet she couldn't force herself to set down the blurry page, lest something happen to it.

In the corner of the room the air shimmered, and Annaconda whirled in time to see her young apprentice step through a small portal. "You're late," she snapped.

The girl bowed. White hair spilled forward from her hood. "My apologies, Your Darkness."

"I'll let it pass . . . this time." Truth be told, Annaconda was glad to share the poem with someone. "I want you to read this and tell me what you make of it."

With only a slight hesitation, the girl accepted the damp paper from Annaconda's clammy outstretched hand. She held it up to the window, reading the backward writing reflected in the glass.

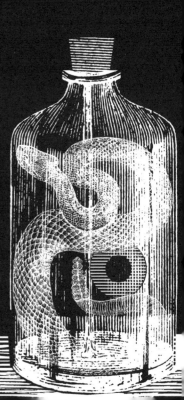

"Well?" Annaconda said impatiently.

"It appears to be a riddle," the girl replied. "About an All-Seeing Eye."

"Of course it's a riddle! But what does it *mean*?" Annaconda snatched back the page. "I haven't slept a wink all night. These words keep taunting me! Surely they must mean *something*!"

"Your Darkness, is this part of my lesson?" the girl asked innocently. "If it is, I'm afraid I don't know the answer."

Annaconda snorted. "My nephew says he found it in the hedge maze. Did you happen to see him last night?"

"Yes, Your Darkness. I was following him. Just as you requested."

"Did you see him carrying a journal? A book? Full of backward-written texts just like this one?"

The girl shook her head. "No, Your Darkness. He heard my footsteps and he started to chase me. I had to leave the maze to escape being caught. I never saw any book."

"Of course you didn't," Annaconda muttered.

The girl bristled under Annaconda's disdainful tone but said nothing. Instead, she produced a heavy textbook from under her cloak; the cover depicted six interlocking triangles underneath the title *Elementary Dark Magick*. "Will there be time for my lesson today?"

The question aggravated Annaconda even more. "Your precious lessons! It's not like I have important work to do! Very well, then. What is it you want to learn? Black candle magic? Unlucky hexes? Poison brews?"

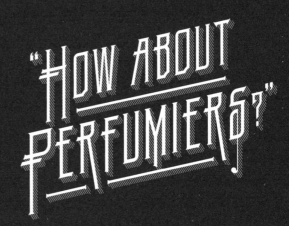

"HOW ABOUT PERFUMIERS?"

asked the apprecntice. Annaconda froze. "What did you say?"

"My textbook has a section on perfumiers. It says that all dark witches must know how to spot them and how to avoid them."

"You needn't worry about perfumiers," Annaconda said. "This hotel is a half day's travel from the nearest village. They'll never find us here."

"Forgive me, Your Darkness, but what are they?"

Annaconda groaned. "Fine. *Fine!* We'll discuss perfumiers." She looked down at the page and shuddered as if dredging up a forgotten memory. The book depicted a beautiful woman with floral tattoos covering her arms and legs. "If you happen to encounter a perfumier—which is highly unlikely—you'll immediately recognize her because of these tattoos. She earns

A PERFUMIER

one flower for every witch she captures. The best perfumiers have hundreds."

"But why do they capture us?"

"Because they are so-called good witches. Powered by white magic and a desire to help people. Can you imagine? It's ridiculous! Why would anyone want to help? These vile creatures can *smell* dark magic. They walk into a room and can sniff out a witch."

"How awful!" said the apprentice.

"Even worse," Annaconda continued, "perfumiers know we're vulnerable when we cast spells, so that's when they strike. They use their magic to draw us into tiny perfume bottles, trapping us forever like genies in a lamp."

"What should I do if I see one?" asked the apprentice.

But that was a topic for another day. The clock on the mantel chimed and Annaconda released a low growl. "We're out of time. I have visitors arriving this afternoon and I must attend to them. In the meantime, I need you to keep track of my nephew. Watch what he's up to. Become his friend."

"You wish for me to talk to him?"

"Yes. The boy's been wandering around an empty hotel for five years. His only friends are a dimwitted chef and an old fool in the library. He hasn't seen another child in years. So act nice and I bet he'll tell you everything he knows."

The apprentice hesitated. "Doesn't that seem a little . . . cruel?"

Annaconda stormed toward her in a rage. "Cruel?! You're here to learn dark magic! *All* dark magic is cruel! That's why it's *dark*! Now get out of here before I lose my temper and transform into a—"

"Yes, Your Darkness,"

the apprentice interrupted quickly, bowing in respect. She immediately opened a portal and vanished through the wall.

Chapter VII.

△

· IN WHICH ·

WARREN

MEETS THE

TRIANGLE

COVEN

s Warren left Mr. Friggs and exited the library, he paused to consider his next steps. He needed to find the journal, but who had taken it? He wondered if he should check the chimney. Maybe one of those pesky ravens had picked it up, and now the birds were pulling out the pages to cushion their nest!

Before Warren could do anything, the hotel intercom crackled to life and Annaconda's voice squawked through the static. "Warren! Lobby! Now!!"

Clearly, she had discovered he'd escaped the boiler room, and she didn't sound happy about it. Warren trudged downstairs as though he was about to meet his doom. Now that he knew Annaconda was a witch, he was more frightened of her than ever. What punishments would she invent to torment him this time?

When he reached the lobby, Warren was surprised to see his aunt flanked by two other women. "There he is, the little weasel," Annaconda said with a sneer. "Warren, come and meet your new aunts."

"My new aunts?"

"That's right, these are my beautiful sisters. They've come to stay with us."

It seemed clear to Warren that witchcraft ran in the family—the two sisters studied him with sinister expressions. "Nice to meet you," he said. He figured that in this case telling a lie was safer than the truth.

The first woman was short and wide, with frizzy gray hair; when she grinned at him, Warren could see she had two missing teeth. "This is Scalene, my elder sister," Annaconda said.

The other woman was curvier and taller, though not quite as tall as his aunt Annaconda. She had long red hair that fell to her ankles and a large hooked nose that was spattered with freckles. "And this is my younger sister, Isosceles."

"You warned us he was ugly," Scalene said, "but he's even more hideous than I expected. He looks like a toad!"

Warren gritted his teeth. He thought this was a case of the pot calling the kettle black, but his father had taught him never to insult a guest—even one who was an evil witch.

"What brings you to our hotel?" Warren asked.

"Just a family visit," Annaconda replied, batting her eyelashes innocently.

"So they're here to help you find the All-Seeing Eye?" Warren asked.

Scalene cackled. "Well, isn't he a bold one!"

"Hmph. Is it *that* obvious?" said Isosceles, pouting.

"What a clever boy," Annaconda added scornfully. "Yes, they are going to assist me. Especially now that I have such a vital clue in my possession." She patted her dress pocket, where Warren knew the page was tucked safely away. "They're also going to help me find the rest of the journal . . . unless you happen to remember where you put it?"

"I told you, I don't have it," Warren said.

Annaconda frowned. "That's a shame. Perhaps my sisters will be able to prod your memory."

All of a sudden, a blinding burst of purplish light filled room and the air reeked of rotten eggs. Warren was astonished to see that his new aunts were no longer themselves: Scalene had transformed into a mangy wolf, and Isosceles into a sharp-beaked vulture!

Annaconda smiled and crossed her arms over her chest. "Meet the members of my triangle coven! Our spirit animals would love the chance to feast upon your flesh!"

Scalene fixed her green-eyed gaze upon Warren and snarled viciously. With jagged

teeth bared, she began skulking toward him. Isosceles flapped her wings, rising over Warren's head and pecking at his golden curls. "Leave me alone!" he cried, stumbling in horror, his arms flailing.

Annaconda threw her head back and cackled. "Not so clever now, are you?"

"Join us, sister!" Isosceles crowed. "Show Warren *your* spirit animal!"

But Annaconda shook her head. She could hear Rupert's heavy footsteps on the stairs. "I mustn't transform myself now; my foolish husband is coming. Change yourselves back, my sisters—quickly!"

Warren sighed in relief. He didn't know what Annaconda's spirit animal was, but he suspected her name offered a pretty big clue. With another burst of purple light and a blast of sulfur stench, Scalene and Isosceles reverted to their human selves mere seconds before Rupert strolled in, his nose buried in a newspaper.

He looked up and sniffed. "Is someone boiling eggs?"

Anaconda swept her husband into a romantic embrace. "Darling! My sweet Prince Charming! I have wonderful news. My lovely sisters have come to visit us!"

During introductions, the sisters preened and fussed over their brother-in-law, straightening his tie, pinching his cheeks, and complimenting his looks.

"So handsome!" cried Isosceles. "Sister didn't tell us she'd married an actor!"

"And a successful businessman to boot," Scalene cooed. "Look at this gorgeous hotel he's running!"

Warren didn't think his uncle's face could possibly get any redder. "M-m-most charmed, ladies!" he stammered. "We'll certainly enjoy your company."

"Darling nephew!" Annaconda called. "Be a good little bellhop and bring my sisters' luggage to their room." She smiled pleasantly but her eyes were dark little pinpoints. Warren just nodded as Scalene and Isosceles heaped suitcases, boxes, and

bags into his arms. They topped off the stack with a cauldron that weighed almost as much as he did.

Warren could barely stand beneath the weight of all the luggage, let alone see over the top. He weaved back and forth, attempting to keep his balance, the bags teetering dangerously.

"Room 805," Annaconda said. "Now, run along."

"But the hotel is empty," Warren said. "Perhaps your sisters would be more comfortable on a lower floor?"

"What?" Annaconda said. "And deprive them of a beautiful view? After they've come all this way? I think not, Warren! Take their bags to Room 805 so they can enjoy our majestic scenery!"

"And be careful!" Scalene snapped.

"THOSE BAGS ARE FRAGILE!"

Chapter VIII.

💀

· IN WHICH ·

WARREN

ENCOUNTERS

A

GHOST

Warren couldn't remember the last time he had to prepare for a guest. He always hoped he could take his time and enjoy the experience. Upon looking around, however, he saw that Annaconda had ransacked the room. The beds were askew; the toppled nightstand was emptied of its contents; the closet doors were pulled off their hinges. Even worse, the room smelled sour, like sweaty socks left too long in a drawer.

Warren set to work, spreading the heavy drapes and pulling open the windows to let in fresh air. He arranged the furniture and cleaned up the mess. Once the beds were remade with fresh linens and fluffy quilts, the room looked much improved. Warren wished he had little mints to place upon the pillows. That would be a nice touch.

The bathroom was tidier. Warren checked the faucets to see if they worked. The water was a little rusty, but after a minute or so it ran clear. He filled a pitcher and set

arren climbed the stairs slowly, knees buckling and arms straining. He could hear the women cackling as they showered Rupert with more flattery and praise. The tower of suitcases seemed ready to topple at any moment, but somehow Warren managed to keep everything in place; after much huffing and puffing, he reached the eighth floor and stumbled to the threshold of Room 805. He kicked open the door just in time; the bags quickly tumbled out of his arms and spilled into the room.

it on the nightstand between the beds, then nodded with satisfaction at a job well done.

As Warren slipped out of the room and back into the hallway, his stomach rumbled. He still hadn't eaten, and it was well past lunchtime. He decided to venture to the kitchen to grab a snack from Chef Bunion, but he didn't dare pass Annaconda and her sisters. He decided to use the dumbwaiter and bypass the lobby altogether.

Warren turned the corner but then stopped in his tracks. A dark form was crouched at the entrance to the dumbwaiter. It seemed to be sniffing the scent of Chef's cooking drifting up the shaft. Sensing a presence, the figure whirled around and rose to full height.

IT WAS

PALEFACE!

Warren knew he was supposed to be courteous and accommodating, but the sight of this frightening person was too much to bear. The face looked sinister, almost inhuman.

Warren turned and bolted down the hall. To his horror, he heard muffled breathing and heavy footsteps rushing after him. He was being chased!

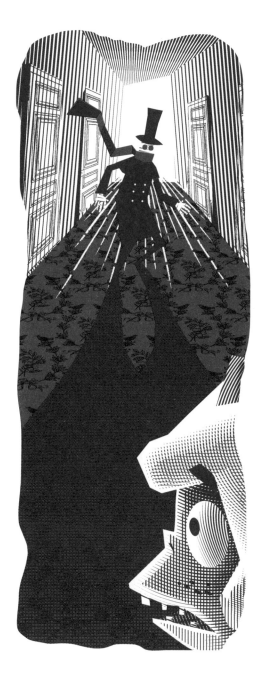

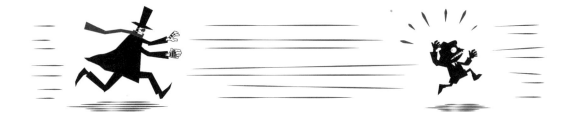

Warren's panic pushed his legs faster as he raced down the hall, swooshing past a painting of a mighty stallion leaping over a turnip patch and a bookshelf that held nothing but Annaconda's fashion magazines. He turned corner after corner, causing the threadbare carpet to buckle and slide in his attempts to outrun his pursuer. But every time Warren dared to glance back, he saw Paleface close behind, tracking him like a bloodhound.

With relief, Warren spotted the stairway up ahead. He leapt onto the bannister and slid to the seventh floor. Paleface's feet pounded down the steps, two at a time. Warren's lungs were bursting as he hurtled down the hall, almost colliding with a bronze statue of a fox on the run. Warren felt just like the fox; his body was tiring and he knew he couldn't maintain this breakneck speed much longer.

Suddenly, he caught a flash of white out of the corner of his eye and an icy hand curled around his wrist. The next thing Warren knew, he was being tugged into the hotel's sewing room, the door slamming shut behind him.

Standing there was the girl from the maze. With a flick of the wrist she slid the dead bolt in place and then raised a pale finger to her lips. "Shhhhh!"

The sewing room was deserted. No one had used its equipment in a very long time. Dusty bobbins of once brightly colored threads hung from pegs on the wall, and bolts of moth-eaten fabric were piled on a nearby shelf. In the middle of the room was an ancient sewing machine atop a rickety table.

Warren could hear Paleface's footsteps in the hallway, and more muffled breathing, but eventually the sounds faded. He slumped to the floor, his heart pounding in the silence.

"You smell terrible," said the girl.

"Excuse me?"

"I'm sorry," she said, waving a hand in front of her nose, "but you smell like rotten eggs!"

Warren remembered the transformation of Scalene and Isosceles and realized that his clothing had absorbed some of their putrid-smelling dark magic.

"It's not me, it's—" he started to explain but then realized it was too strange. The girl would think he was crazy. "Who are you, anyway? I feel like you've been haunting me since last night."

The girl drew back, looking cross. "Haunting is a bit of an exaggeration. I may be pale, but I'm certainly no ghost! My name is Petula."

Pale was an understatement. The girl was white from head to toe. The only hint of color came from her clear blue eyes. Petula was almost as unusual looking as Warren. He decided he liked her immediately.

"I'm Warren the 13th." He held out his hand. "Truce?"

Petula considered him for a moment, then shook his hand. "Truce."

Without further ado, Warren's stomach released an embarrassing grumble. "You must be hungry," the girl said, reaching into her pocket for a bit of ham sandwich wrapped in wax paper. "I nicked this from

the kitchen. Here, you can have the rest."

Warren accepted the sandwich gratefully and noticed that all the crust had been nibbled off. He shrugged and bit into it anyway. He was too hungry to be picky.

"Are you here alone?" Warren asked.

"No, silly. My mother and I are staying here. We arrived yesterday morning."

Warren didn't see how that was possible. The only guest to arrive yesterday morning was Paleface. If there had been any other arrivals, surely Rupert would have called him to assist with the luggage.

"We're taking an extended holiday," Petula said. "Don't ask me why we chose this hotel, because there is absolutely nothing to do. You don't even have a swimming pool!"

"You're certainly finding ways to stay busy," Warren said. "I saw you in the hedge maze last night, sneaking around. Was scaring me your idea of a joke?"

"I'm sorry," Petula said. "It's so awfully boring around here. I was only trying to have a little fun."

"What about the boiler room this morning? Are you the one who unlocked the door?"

Petula nodded. "What on earth were you doing in there anyway?"

"My aunt locked me in."

"How dreadful!"

Warren shrugged. He'd grown accustomed to Annaconda's cruelty, but he appreciated Petula's concern. It was nice to talk to someone his own age. He began telling her all about his aunt and her evil sisters and their plan to steal the All-Seeing Eye.

"But that's not fair!" Petula said. "If the treasure really exists, it sounds like your ancestors wanted *you* to have it. Not some stranger who married your uncle a few months ago."

Warren shook his head sadly. "If I try to stop them, they'll use dark magic to make my life miserable. Scalene can turn into a wolf, Isosceles can turn into a vulture, and Annaconda . . . well, you can probably imagine what she can turn into."

Petula shivered. "I hate snakes."

"Me, too," Warren said. "So you see, there's nothing I can do."

"Sure, there is," said Petula. "You just have to find the journal before they do."

"But I've looked everywhere!"

"Then you'll have to look everywhere all over again," Petula said. "But this time I'll help you. We can hunt for it together."

Warren was struck by the kindness of her offer. First Sketchy and now Petula—he couldn't remember the last time he'd made two friends in one day!

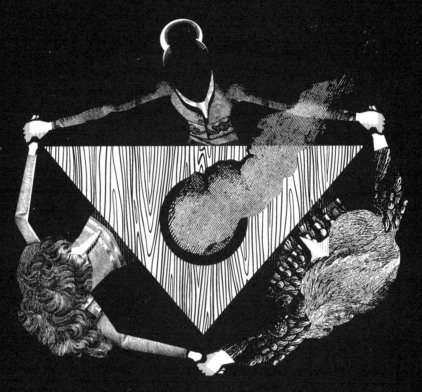

The triangle coven sat around a table in Annaconda's room, scheming to recover the lost book and decipher its text. "We must spread out and search every room thoroughly," Annaconda said. "The journal must be here somewhere!"

"But the hotel is so big and there are so many rooms," Scalene said with a moan. She was almost as lazy as Uncle Rupert.

"Perhaps we could convince our ugly little nephew to search on our behalf," Isosceles suggested.

"Fools!" Annaconda snapped. "The reason I summoned you here was so that *you* could help! Besides, I would never trust the boy to turn over the journal if he found it."

"I say we skip the book and head straight for the treasure!" said Scalene. "That's what I'm interested in!"

Annaconda shook her head. "Listen, you lackwits. I've spent the past four months searching in vain for the All-Seeing Eye. This pathetic page is the closest thing I've found that hints of its whereabouts; the rest of the journal is the key. If you're unwilling to put in the effort and help me find it, then pack up and *leave*!"

Isosceles squawked. "And let you have the treasure all for yourself? Ha!"

"That's right," Scalene said. "I'm not going anywhere until I get my fair share. I can't very well return to the pub empty-handed. I told everyone I was coming to get it!"

"*Whaaaat* did you say?" Annaconda's eyes narrowed into slits.

"Everyone is expecting me to return with an amazing treasure!" Scalene said, rolling her eyes as though the situation were obvious. "I can't let them down."

Annaconda quaked with rage. "You told an entire restaurant...," she grated through tightly clenched teeth, "full of people . . . about the All-Seeing Eye?"

"Well, I couldn't just leave without telling them where I was going!" said Scalene, offended. "I'm a regular!"

"And you," Annaconda turned, setting her sights on Isosceles. "I hope *you* had more sense than your sister. Tell me you kept our plans a secret."

"You never *said* it was a secret," Isosceles said, frowning. "You should have told us it was a secret!"

It was implied." Annaconda roared. "And how many people did you brag to?"

"I wouldn't call it bragging exactly," Isosceles shot back. "I was simply sharing exciting news with people I'm close to

MY NEIGHBORS.
MY HAIRDRESSER.
MY POSTMAN.
MY MAID.

Oh, and my livery driver and my—"

"Enough!" Annaconda interrupted. "Let's hope no one believed your tall tales. I take comfort in knowing that only a fool would be crazy enough to come all this way—"

Annaconda's own rant was interrupted by the crackle of the intercom. "Warren!!!" Rupert's voice wailed. "Lobby, please, straightaway! We have new guests! *Lots* of new guests!"

Chapter IX.

· IN WHICH ·

WARREN

IS

VERY, VERY, VERY

BUSY

arren could hear the alarm in Uncle Rupert's voice. He and Petula quickly unlocked the sewing room door and scrambled downstairs. When they arrived in the lobby, Warren was astonished at the sight. The room was packed with guests, well over a hundred, all shouting and jostling to check in at the front desk.

Beyond the double doors was an even bigger crowd vying to get inside. Warren had never seen so many different kinds of people—it was as if they had come from all over the world. He wanted to speak with each and every one, to hear stories about where they were from and what they had seen. It was all tremendously exciting.

As he and Petula pushed through the throng, they overheard snippets of conversations; the most frequently repeated words were "treasure" and "eye." A woman dressed in a fancy gown was digging in a planter. A man in a surgeon's coat was using a sharp metal tool to pry up a loose tile. A stout hobo in a tattered suit had managed to elbow his way behind the desk and was using his bindle to jimmy open a file cabinet. Rupert was occupied with trying to push him out.

"My goodness!" Petula exclaimed.

"Where did all these people come from?" Warren asked.

"Help!" Rupert cried.

Warren hurried over and tried to calm his uncle. "Just handle the people one at a time," he said. "Everyone will have to take turns checking in." Then Warren raised his voice above the din, asking the guests to form an orderly line. It took several minutes and much pushing and shoving but eventually they obeyed his request.

At the head of the line was a burly man in a khaki safari outfit. He pounded rudely on the desk. "*Ahem!* Excuse me! My family and I require a room!"

"Yes, right away!" Rupert cried as he fumbled for a key. "Warren, see to their bags!"

As Warren rushed to assist, he noticed the family was rather large; in addition to the father there were a scowling mother holding twin babies, two older girls, and a chubby boy about Warren's age. The entire group was dressed in similar fashion, sporting pantaloon-like shorts and pith helmets, all except the infants.

"O-ho! A wild beast!" the boy exclaimed upon seeing Warren. "May I hunt it, Father?"

"As you wish," the man said.

The boy unholstered a toy rifle, aimed it at Warren, and pulled the trigger. It made a soft *pop!* and a tiny cork pelted Warren in the chest.

"Ow!" Warren cried. "That hurt!"

"I've wounded it, Father! May I hunt it again?"

"As you wish," the father said again with a sigh.

The family's luggage smelled like moldy leather and elephant dung. The bags felt like lead, full of clanking pots and pans, and Warren struggled to carry everything up the stairs. No one offered to help. And even worse, the boy kept firing at Warren until they arrived at their room. Bidding the family farewell, Warren hurried downstairs.

As the hotel's only bellhop, Warren spent the rest of the afternoon helping people check into their rooms. Most of the guests were unbearably rude, and each one demanded that he help them in their quest.

Next in line was a wealthy jeweler, his hands adorned with sparkly rings; he flashed a phony smile and waved a banknote under Warren's nose. "Don't bother showing me to my room," he said. "Simply direct me to the All-Seeing Eye. I hear it is the most beautiful jewel in the world, and I simply must have it for my collection!"

The woman was followed by a husband-and-wife team of circus acrobats dressed in matching silver bodysuits. They believed the All-Seeing Eye was a pair of spectacles that would forever improve their vision. When Warren refused to help with their search, they hung him by his suspenders from the lobby chandelier. He spent the next twenty minutes dangling midair and trying to break free.

Next came a humpbacked white-haired woman who smelled like roses. She told Warren the All-Seeing Eye was an enchanted crystal ball that could see far into the future; all she wanted was to steal a quick glance. When Warren explained he was unable to grant her request, her rosy-cheeked smile turned into a scowl. Wagging a bony finger, she screeched: "A curse upon you!" Warren half expected lightning bolts to spring from her old wrinkled hands. [Thankfully none did.]

To a barbarian draped in musty furs, the All-Seeing Eye was an enchanted rock that could crush his enemies. When Warren repeated [for the hundredth time] that he didn't know where to find it, the man let out a mighty battle cry, picked Warren up, and threw him out the window. Fortunately, the lobby was on the ground floor. Warren landed in a cluster of bushes, shaken but unharmed.

Under normal circumstances, Warren would be the first to say that impolite guests were better than no guests at all. But the mania about the All-Seeing Eye made him nervous. Beating Annaconda and her sisters to the treasure would be challenging enough; now dozens of fortune seekers were joining the race. Guests streamed in from all parts of the globe. Some were poor and desperate, others were wealthy and leisured, regarding the search for the Eye as some sort of sport. There were hunters and explorers, performers and artists, conmen and scholars and commoners and aristocrats. All of them had a different idea about the All-Seeing Eye.

BUT WHICH OF THEM WAS
RIGHT?

Halfway through the afternoon, Anaconda pushed into the lobby, studying the crowd with horrified curiosity. Rupert interpreted her gaping expression as a joyful sort of shock. "Isn't it wonderful, my love?" he shouted, giving her a jolly wave from across the room. "Business is booming! I'll shower you with all the gifts your beauty deserves!"

Annaconda smiled thinly before shooting Warren a withering look, as if the bedlam were all his fault. She stormed out without saying a word. Even Petula—who earlier seemed so desperate for something to do— had grown weary of the commotion and drifted off in search of quieter diversions.

Warren worked nonstop, carrying luggage and admitting guests to their rooms. By sunset Rupert was passed out at his desk, too exhausted even to drag himself over to the red velvet couch. Warren dreamed of crawling into his much-needed bed, but before he could retire to the attic, the lobby's double doors creaked open and one last guest stepped inside. The man was short and thickset, with a wiry black beard, a patch over one eye, and a wooden peg leg. His pants were tattered at the hems but he wore a military-style coat, the woolen fabric studded with smart-looking buttons. "Arrrgh," he said in greeting. "Sorry I be late! I couldn't decide where to dock me ship."

Warren stood gaping. It was his first look at a real honest-to-goodness pirate!

"Welcome," Warren said, finding his voice. "You're in luck—we still have a couple rooms left." He scurried forward to help the pirate with his luggage, which consisted of a heavy wooden trunk latched with a padlock. Warren tugged at the handle but the trunk weighed too much; its bottom scraped loudly across the lobby floor. Despite all the ruckus, Rupert continued sleeping soundly, a testament to his exhaustion or his laziness, or possibly both.

"Yar, has anyone found this All-Seeing Aye?" asked the pirate.

"I believe it's the All-Seeing *Eye*," Warren corrected. "Spelled with an 'e.'"

"That's what I said!"

Warren lifted the trunk onto his back, preparing to carry it up several flights of stairs. "No one's found it yet," he explained. "No one can even agree about what it is."

"I've no confusion on that point!" the pirate exclaimed. "Everyone knows it be a magical compass. The aye will guide you through any fog, lead you out of the belly of any sea serpent, and direct you to the greatest fortunes."

"That's as good a guess as any," Warren said. He then introduced himself and offered to show the pirate to his room.

"Pleased to meet ye, Warren—

Me name be Captain GRAYISHWHITISHBEARD!"

The name caught Warren by surprise. Rather than grayish and whitish, the captain's beard was a deep dark black. The pirate noticed his confusion and grinned. "I know what ye be thinking," he whispered conspiratorially. "Truth be, I dye me beard to appear young and hale!"

"It looks good," Warren said.

They headed upstairs, with Warren pausing on the landing between the fifth and sixth floors to catch his breath.

"Here, lad, let me take over," said the captain, reaching for his trunk. "I know it be heavy."

"No, sir!" Warren said. "It's my job. I can do it."

"Arrr, I like a lad who's not afraid of hard work! Ye would make a good first mate on me ship!"

Warren's eyes bulged. "Really? Do you think so?"

"I know so!" the captain exclaimed. "I've been doing this profession all me life. I know potential when I sees it."

Warren allowed himself to daydream for just a moment. How much fun would it be to travel the world on a pirate ship! Imagine the adventures: discovering hidden islands, dancing jigs, blasting cannons at sea monsters. It all sounded so exotic and exciting.

"Is it fun being a pirate?" Warren asked.

"A pirate?" The captain looked befuddled and scratched his beard. "Can't say I know! I've never met one!"

"But . . . then what . . ."

The captain let out a hearty laugh that reverberated through the halls. A guest in Room 514 opened the door and hissed, "Shhhhh!"

"You think I be a pirate?" he said. "Lad, I hope ye never have to cross paths with a real one! Pirates be fearsome souls! They ride the seas hunting for treasure with their wild eyes, unruly beards, and missing limbs. They be truly a force to be reckoned with!"

Warren thought this description fit Captain Grayishwhitishbeard, but he kept this thought to himself.

"No lad, I be no pirate. I be an importer exporter!" He paused and again scratched his beard. "Well, more importer than exporter. Mostly importer."

Soon they reached the captain's room on the seventh floor, and Warren was stunned when the man reached into his coat pocket and handed him a gold doubloon! Warren hadn't received a tip in years. He closed his fingers over the coin, squeezing to make sure it was real.

"Thank you!" Warren said.

"No, thank *ye*, lad," the captain said with a grin. "There's more where that came from if ye'd like to join me crew."

Warren realized the man was offering him a job. Leaving the hotel behind seemed unimaginable but . . .

. . . to be an importer exporter! To live a life of adventure like Jacques Rustyboots! To see the world and meet new people and get away from Aunt Annaconda! Warren knew chances like that don't come along every day.

"I'll think about it," he said at last.

And that night Warren placed the doubloon under his pillow and sank into a deep restful sleep, his dreams filled with high adventure on the rolling seas.

The next morning Annaconda chose to take breakfast in her room. The idea of dining amongst a hotel full of guests seemed most unpleasant. Isosceles and Scalene sat beside her, gobbling eggs benedict and golden hash browns, which Warren had sent up via the dumbwaiter upon learning of the arrangement.

"This is all your fault!" Annaconda snapped at her sisters. "If you hadn't opened your big mouths we wouldn't be in this predicament!"

"Sister, you need to stay calm," Scalene said. "Think of it this way: the more people are looking for the Eye, the more quickly it will be found."

"And then we'll just take it from them!" Isosceles added with a cackle. "Easy-peasy!"

In the corner of the room, the air began to shimmer like an oasis in the desert. Suddenly a black portal materialized and a figure dressed in a black robe stepped through. The girl bowed reverently.

"Ah, my apprentice!" Annaconda said. "You're just in time for today's lesson."

"You have an apprentice?" Scalene asked, clearly jealous.

"Your apprentice can draw portals?"

Isosceles said, even more jealous.

"My young apprentice puts the two of you to shame!" Annaconda turned her attention to the girl. "Have you charmed my nephew yet?"

"I introduced myself yesterday," the black-clad girl replied. "We spent the afternoon helping guests check in. I must confess, Your Darkness, I think the boy is telling the truth. He doesn't know where the journal is. Someone must have stolen it from him."

"But who?" Annaconda said. "Who else would be wandering the hedge maze in the middle of the night?"

"I am trying to find out, Your Darkness."

Scalene studied the apprentice with envy. "Oh, how I miss having magic. Can you cast any spells besides portals?"

"A few," the apprentice replied cryptically.

"Never mind other spells!" Annaconda railed, turning back to the girl. "I want you to spend the day with my nephew. Keep close to him. And when he finds the journal, bring it to me immediately!"

"I am your humble servant," the apprentice said, bowing in retreat.

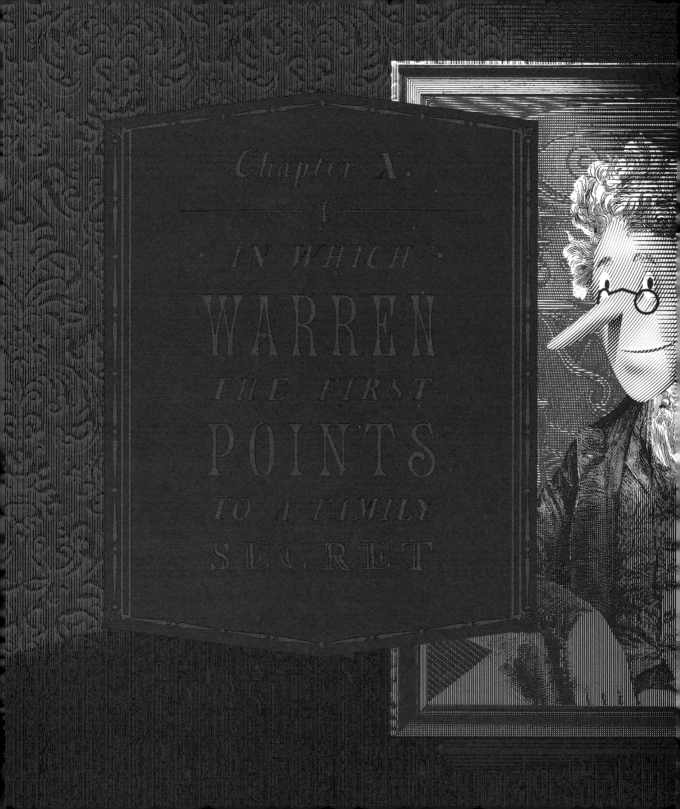

Chapter X.

IN WHICH WARREN THE FIRST POINTS TO A FAMILY SECRET

 arren had never experienced such a busy breakfast. With so many guests ordering so much food, Chef Bunion moved in a blur, cracking eggs, flipping pancakes, buttering toast, and pressing grapefruits. Warren was equally busy. He scurried from table to table with stacks of trays, passing out fluffy omelets and mounds of bacon and fresh-squeezed juice. Fights broke out in the dining hall as guests scrambled for the choicest cuts of ham. Bowls were dropped, glasses were shattered, coffee was spilled. A plate flew like a discus across the room, passing within an inch of Warren's head. This was nothing like the elegant and civilized breakfasts that Warren remembered from childhood. This was pandemonium!

Warren was hoping to find time after the morning service to search for the journal, but he was delayed by guests asking for a million different things:

"Is there a wrench I can use?"

"Can someone unlock this door?"

"Do you have a map of the grounds?"

Evidence of destruction was everywhere. Vases were smashed, canvases were torn, vents were wedged open and tossed carelessly aside. If Warren had been annoyed by Annaconda's destruction, the disarray caused by the new guests nearly drove him mad! They lacked all restraint. A man had used a claw hammer to chip through a bathtub.

A woman with a trowel was excavating the front lawn. Another woman had stepped into one of the holes, and now she complained of a twisted ankle. With every new crisis, Warren felt himself growing angrier and angrier. His father always treated guests politely regardless of the circumstances, but this was ridiculous!

The final straw came when Warren found guests vandalizing the hedge maze. At first it seemed harmless enough: a few people hopelessly lost had clawed through the brambles in an attempt to escape. But soon everybody was hacking at branches and slashing shortcuts through the shrubbery. A few were even digging trenches to crawl underneath.

Warren heard the roar of a motorized saw and rushed to the center of the maze. There he found a lumberjack about to slice through a beautiful specimen bush.

"STOP, STOP, STOP!"

he cried, throwing himself in front of the blade.

"Outta my way!" growled the man.

"I've had quite enough!" Warren said. "If you want to cut through the hedges, you'll have to go through me first!"

For a moment, the lumberjack seemed to consider the idea—but then he thought better of it. "Crazy kid," he snarled and stalked off.

Warren exhaled with relief. His victory was small, but it was a victory nonetheless. He exited the maze and returned to the hotel, where he proceeded to clean up one mess after another. At this rate, he'd never have a chance to search for the Eye.

Warren was sweeping plaster on the fifth floor when Petula approached in a rush. "This is awful," she said. "Your guests are running wild!"

"It's worse than awful," said Warren. "Every time I start looking for the journal, I'm interrupted by—"

But again he was interrupted, this time by a loud clatter. Down the hall, the gentleman jeweler was fighting the fur-be-decked barbarian; the former had dared slap the latter across the cheek with his elegant white gloves. The barbarian retaliated by grabbing the jeweler, raising him over his head, and throwing him into a grandfather clock. The ancient family heirloom smashed to the floor.

Just then the library door opened and out ran a group of teenagers. Mr. Friggs chased after them, shaking his cane and yelling unintelligibly through toothless gums. Warren and Petula helped him back into the room and then barricaded the door with a chair. Petula plucked the missing dentures off the floor, brushing them off before returning them to their owner.

"This is terrible! Just terrible!" said Mr. Friggs, tears springing to his eyes. "I've been guarding the library all day! My precious books!"

Warren looked around in dismay. The room had always been cluttered, but it was an organized sort of clutter that seemed to make sense, at least to its occupant. Now the place was in shambles, torn books and loose pages scattered all about.

"I'm sorry, Mr. Friggs," Warren said. "I'm doing my best to control the situation, but I can't be in a hundred places at once."

"Your father would be heartsick to see what has become of his beloved hotel! It's a travesty!" cried Mr. Friggs. Warren and Petula helped him into his chair and made him a cup of tea. Normally the beverage was just the thing to soothe his jagged nerves, but today he was too distressed. "If this madness goes on much longer, the whole place will be ruined!"

"Don't worry," Warren said with renewed determination. "I'm going to find the journal, and I'm going to find the Eye, and I'm going to get our hotel back to the way it used to be!"

"I just hope it's not too late," Mr. Friggs muttered, gazing into his chipped teacup.

"Stay here and keep the door locked,"

Warren said. "We'll take care of everything."

Upon leaving the library, Petula turned to Warren. "Where are we going?"

"You'll probably think this is a little strange," he said, "but there's someone I like to talk to whenever I have a problem."

As they descended the stairs to the Hall of Ancestors, Warren braced himself for even more destruction. But to his immense relief, he saw that the gallery had mostly been spared. Paintings were removed from their hooks and some of the paper backings were shredded, but none of the portraits had been harmed beyond repair.

Beginning with the painting of Warren the 1st, Warren the 13th walked down the hallway and carefully rehung each one. His forefathers seemed to glare back in dissatisfaction. Warren the 1st had always looked stern and angry, but today even jolly Warren the 6th's goofy smile seemed pained.

"Who are these people?" Petula asked.

"These are my ancestors," Warren explained. "Warren the 1st designed the hotel, and Warren the 2nd built it. Warren the 3rd and all the other Warrens took care of it during their lifetimes. Now it's my turn."

At last Warren reached the portrait of his father. Warren the 12th was lying facedown on the floor, the frame's paper backing slashed and ripped open; no doubt someone was hoping to find the treasure tucked inside. Warren gently lifted the portrait and turned it around, bracing for the worst. He was relieved to see his father's kindly face intact.

"I'm sorry, Dad," Warren whispered softly. "Things are so crazy and I don't know what to do. I wish someone would give me a clue."

The portrait stared back with caring, patient eyes.

"That's odd," Petula said.

"I know it's strange," Warren said, feeling embarrassed, "but sometimes talking to him makes me feel better."

"Not *that*, silly. *This!*" Petula was pointing at the portrait of Warren the 2nd. "This is the man who wrote the journal, right?"

"Yes. His father was a military general, but he was an architect."

The portrait showed Warren Jr. seated at his desk, his arm resting casually on a pile of papers. He wore a quizzical expression and his hair stuck out at odd angles. Wireframe glasses were propped on the bridge of his long nose, giving him a wizardly air.

"Look at the portraits side by side," Petula said. "Doesn't it look like Warren the 1st is pointing at Warren the 2nd?"

Warren scurried over and examined the paintings more carefully. Petula was right: the hand of Warren the 1st was tucked inside his jacket, with his index finger aimed decidedly in the direction of Warren the 2nd.

"It could just be a coincidence," Petula said. "It might not mean anything—"

"No, I think it does," Warren murmured, concentrating hard. "I think he's trying to show us something. Warren the 1st is pointing at the *desk* of Warren the 2nd!"

Warren had admired the portrait hundreds of times without ever noticing the desk or the document lying atop it.

WARREN THE 2ND

He stepped even closer and realized the paper was an architectural drawing of the hotel. He stepped closer still, nearly pushing his nose against the canvas.

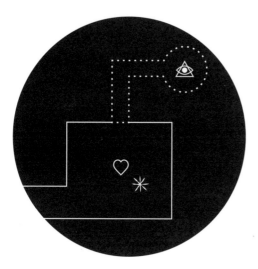

Right there, drawn on the blueprints of the hotel, was the picture of an eye! It couldn't possibly be a coincidence.

"The legends have been true all along!" Petula exclaimed. "The Eye really is hidden somewhere in the hotel!"

"But where?" Warren asked. He knew every inch of the building but didn't recognize the room with the eye. And nothing on the blueprints was labeled. "We're running out of time. The guests are tearing the place apart. Sooner or later one of them is bound to find it!"

Petula pointed to a little heart drawn in the center of a room adjacent to the eye. "Remember the riddle?" She recited the first two lines from memory:

"When the Heart of the Warren hears
The tone played by the rightful hand,
The All-Seeing Eye will appear."

"The Eye must be hidden next to the Heart of the Warren," he said.

But he was still no closer to solving the puzzle. Where in the hotel was the Heart of the Warren?

"What's this other shape?" Warren asked, pointing to the squiggle. "It looks like a star."

"Maybe it's a smudge?" Petula said. "Like the artist made a mistake and tried to cover it up."

Warren didn't think so. Every detail in the painting was perfectly rendered. His ancestors had left him a clear and deliberate clue. If it was a splotch or a squiggle, it had to mean something.

BUT WHAT?

Chapter XI.

IN WHICH

WARREN

AND

PETULA

CONDUCT A

SEARCH

arren and Petula arrived in the kitchen to find Chef Bunion positively frantic. "Let me guess," he said, looking at Petula disapprovingly. "You're here to complain about my cooking!"

"It's okay, Chef," Warren said. "This is my friend Petula. She's helping me with a search."

"And I would never complain about your cooking!" Petula added. "I had one of your omelets this morning and it was delicious!"

The compliment worked wonders. "Please, forgive me," Chef Bunion said, taking a deep breath. "I'm under a great deal of stress. Most of our guests are simply awful! They insult my food even as they demand more, more, more! Then they come in here raiding my pantries for so-called treasure! I'd like to put them on a strict all-porridge diet!"

"That wouldn't be much of a punishment," Warren said. "Even your porridge is pretty tasty."

"Well, it's the cinnamon," Chef Bunion said proudly. "Just a pinch in every pot and the flavor is transformed."

"I love cinnamon," Petula said. "I'm going to try the porridge tomorrow morning."

"I'll serve you a special bowl of it myself," Chef promised. "Nice and warm!"

All the praise improved Chef's mood tremendously, and he began preparing dinner with his usual care and good humor. "Now what's this about a search?"

"We're looking for an old journal," Warren said. "A leather-bound book with pages falling out. I don't suppose you've seen it?"

"As a matter of fact," Chef said, tapping his chin with a spatula, "I may have seen it yesterday morning, during the breakfast you missed. A rather odd fellow was reading just such a book. I remember him well because of the bandages. Wrapped up like a mummy, he was."

"PALEFACE!"

Warren cried.

Chef shrugged. "I didn't catch his name."

"The night he arrived," Petula said, "he must have followed you into the hedge maze and stolen it!"

"We need to search his room," Warren said. But then he remembered he hadn't escorted Paleface and didn't know which room was his. "We'll check the logbook. Let's go to the front desk."

"Hold on," Chef Bunion said. "You won't get very far on an empty stomach." He passed a fragrant bowl of thick orange-colored liquid under Warren's nose, then offered a serving to Petula. "Roasted pumpkin soup with extra cinnamon for my good friend Warren the 13th and Petula, my new favorite guest!"

Warren and Petula slurped their soup as quickly as possible, then hurried upstairs to the lobby. They found Uncle Rupert standing behind the check-in desk, counting stacks of money and looking very pleased.

"Hello, my boy!" he said cheerfully. "I do say, I'm beginning to see the benefits of running a hotel. All of a sudden the business is quite profitable!"

"You might want to be a little more careful," Warren suggested. "I'm not sure I'd trust all these guests." Given their destructiveness, Warren wasn't sure he trusted *any* of them.

"Don't worry about that, my boy!" Rupert said, making fists and jabbing them like a boxer in the ring. "If anyone tries any funny business, I'll show them who's boss!"

Petula seemed unimpressed with Rupert's macho display. "May we see the logbook?" she asked.

Rupert blinked slowly, as if noticing her for the first time. "And who may I say is asking?"

"This is my friend Petula," Warren said.

"Oh! Young romance blooms!" Rupert exclaimed. "No doubt you've seen the happiness shared by Annaconda and myself, and you long for a love as great as ours!"

"Ugh! No!" Warren cried. "We just want to see the logbook!"

"Come again?" Rupert asked. "The log-what?"

"That doesn't bode well," Petula muttered under her breath.

Warren ducked behind the desk and rooted in the drawers until he located a tattered book embossed with the word "Log."

"Oh, that old thing!" Rupert said. "What do you need that for?"

Warren ignored his uncle's question and began flipping through the pages while Petula peered over his shoulder. "It's blank!" she said.

"Not exactly," Warren said. Rupert may not have bothered to record any guest names or room numbers, but he'd been writing plenty. The pages were filled with hearts and flowery doodles twining around the name "Annaconda" written in loopy script.

Rupert snatched the book away. "Stay out of my diary!" he exclaimed.

"That's not a diary!" Warren said. "It's for recording the names of the hotel's guests! The log is supposed to tell us which room each person is staying in."

"But that's so much work!" exclaimed Rupert. "We have so many rooms with so many guests, I'd be writing all afternoon!"

"Oh, never mind," Warren said. "Just tell us what room you gave to Paleface. You know, the weird guest who's all bandaged up and had only a small red satchel? Remember?"

"Of course I remember. Room 842," Rupert said.

"Thank you," Warren said, heading for the stairs.

"Or maybe it was 248," added Rupert.

"Okay," Petula said to Warren. "I'll check 842 and you check 248."

"Unless I'm confusing him with the barbarian," Rupert continued, "in which case he's in Room 371."

Warren and Petula stared at him in disbelief.

"Or perhaps Room 516 or 615, I always mix those two up." Rupert removed a pencil tucked behind his ear and began writing in the logbook, scribbling daisies around Annaconda's name. "Or maybe 156? I feel certain there was a six . . . "

Warren and Petula plodded up the stairs to the hotel's second floor.

"Your uncle might be the most foolish person I've ever met," Petula said.

"He's just lovesick is all," Warren said. "We'll have to search every floor, but if we work together, it shouldn't take long."

Petula was skeptical. "How many rooms are there?"

"A hundred and thirteen," Warren said. "And every one must be occupied because the key rack is empty."

They decided to split up. Warren took the odd-numbered floors and Petula took the even-numbered floors, and the search lasted most of the afternoon. Warren told each guest that he was part of the hospitality staff. "I'm just checking to see if everything is satisfactory," he'd say, but of course nothing was satisfactory anymore about the Warren Hotel. Every guest had a long list of complaints, and each problem sent Warren scrambling to find a solution.

The farmers in Room 330 protested that the beds were too lumpy. When Warren investigated, he discovered potatoes stuffed under the mattresses. "I think I've found the problem," he said, but the farmers were insulted. They claimed that at home all their mattresses were used for potato storage, and sleeping in the beds was as comfortable as lying on a cloud.

The hobo in Room 504 had made a small fire in the middle of his room. When he answered the door, a plume of smoke curled into the hallway. Warren ran to fill a bucket with water to extinguish the flames, then explained to the man that fires were not permitted in the hotel. The hobo complained that he was cold, so Warren showed him how to turn on the heat.

The safari family was staying in Room 702. The chubby boy took one look at Warren, grabbed his cork gun, and leapt out the door. Warren ran down four flights of stairs and then hid himself in a rusting suit of armor. He waited silently until the boy passed, then emerged from his refuge and resumed his search.

Every new room revealed different signs of destruction. Beds were not only unmade but entirely dismantled. Wardrobes were overturned, nightstands upended. Carpets were peeled back, revealing sharp tacks that pricked Warren's feet through the soles of his shoes. Bathtubs had been shoved into bedrooms so that guests could peer down drainpipes. It took all of Warren's concentration to stay on task. He simply logged everything in his sketchbook and planned to return later to make the repairs.

It was late by the time Petula and Warren finished their search. They compared notes and realized neither had found any sign of Paleface or the missing journal.

"Now what?" Petula said. Circles had formed under her tired eyes.

Warren was exhausted, too. "I guess we get some sleep and try again in the morning. We'll run into him sooner or later."

"Unless he left altogether," Petula said.

Warren's hopes fell. He hadn't thought of that.

Glumly, he said good-night and began making his way to the attic and his tiny cramped room. He paused on the sixth-floor landing, halted by the sound of a loud *thump!* Curious, he crept out of the stairwell and into the adjoining hallway. Most

likely it was just another guest wreaking havoc. Tired as he was, Warren was eager to put a quick stop to the mischief.

But the sound revealed itself to be Captain Grayishwhitishbeard dragging his trunk through the hallway.

"Ahoy!" the captain called.

"Where are you going at this hour?" Warren asked in surprise.

"Alas, I be feeling seasick," he replied. "It's best I go back to me boat."

"Seasick?" Warren repeated. "But we're not at sea." In fact, the nearest ocean was more than a hundred miles away.

The captain shook his head. "No, but the sea be my home, and where ye might be homesick, I be feeling seasick!"

Warren supposed his logic made sense, though he was still disappointed. "But you just got here," he said. "What about the All-Seeing Aye?"

"Yar, there be too much competition and too little benefit. I be feeling cooped up here, and I'd rather seek me fortunes on the open water."

"Then let me help you with your trunk," Warren said. He didn't relish the idea of carrying the chest back down to the lobby, but as the hotel's only bellhop, he knew it was the right thing to do.

"Don't ye worry about it, lad!" the captain said. Grunting, he hoisted the chest onto his back. "Say, why don't ye come with me?"

"What? You mean right now?" Warren said.

"Yar! It will be a grand time! Ye can meet the rest of me crew, and we can set sail for any place ye want to go! Grecko, maybe? Or the Malwoods? Or even the frozen seas of Frostbjorn?"

Warren's heart beat faster as he imagined sitting in the crow's nest of a grand sailing vessel, peering through a pair of binoculars and yelling "Land ho!" Perhaps he could even have his own talking parrot, like McCrackers the macaw from his beloved Jacques Rustyboots books. Captain Grayishwhitishbeard's offer certainly sounded more appealing than a fruitless search for a missing journal, managing a run-down hotel, and serving an endless stream of ungrateful guests.

"Do I need to decide on the spot?" Warren asked.

"I be leaving right now," the captain replied.

As Warren walked down the stairs, past the ripped-up floorboards and peeled-back wallpaper, he wondered if all his hard work

was worth it. Everything seemed to be a lost cause. If the All-Seeing Eye was found by Aunt Annaconda or any of the guests, the hotel would no longer stand. Maybe it was best if he got out now, so he wouldn't have to see his beloved home fall.

Let's face it, Warren thought glumly, the hotel will never return to the way it was when Father was in charge. I've let everyone down. Maybe it's better if I go.

Warren and Captain Grayishwhitishbeard reached the ground floor. Rupert was fast asleep, snoring loudly on the couch. The captain threw open the lobby doors with a grand flourish. "Well, lad? What say ye? Ready for a life of adventure?"

Outside, the forest beckoned and, somewhere beyond it, the sea. Warren's heart was racing. Could he really run away and abandon his home?

"Is there time for me to say goodbye?" Warren asked. He thought about those he'd be leaving behind: Uncle Rupert and Chef Bunion and Mr. Friggs. Even his new friends Sketchy and Petula.

"Sorry, me lad, but the sea waits for no man. Will ye answer the call?"

Warren looked down and saw the hotel's snail trailing across the floor. It was the third or fourth time he'd seen it that day. He didn't know why the creature chose to live indoors; it had shown up some four months earlier and had been creeping around ever since. It lived in a cracked purple shell with yellow spots and a wobbly spiral—not exactly the prettiest, most perfect home, but the tiny mollusk carried it with pride. Warren knelt down and scooped up the snail, speeding its travel across the porch. Then he looked to the captain and announced his decision.

"I wish I could go with you," Warren said. "I've always wanted to see the rest of the world, and you seem like a kind and able captain. But this hotel is my home and I have to take care of it. My ancestors are counting on me."

"I understand, lad," the captain said, ruffling Warren's hair. "Ye can always change your mind. I'll be back this way in, oh, another fifteen years."

Warren's heart sank. "Fifteen years?"

"Maybe fourteen," the captain said with a wink. "If there's wind in me sails."

Warren watched the captain depart, dragging his trunk through the gates and pulling it deep into the forest, until the evening fog obscured him. His best chance for a better life was walking away. Warren hoped he'd made the right choice.

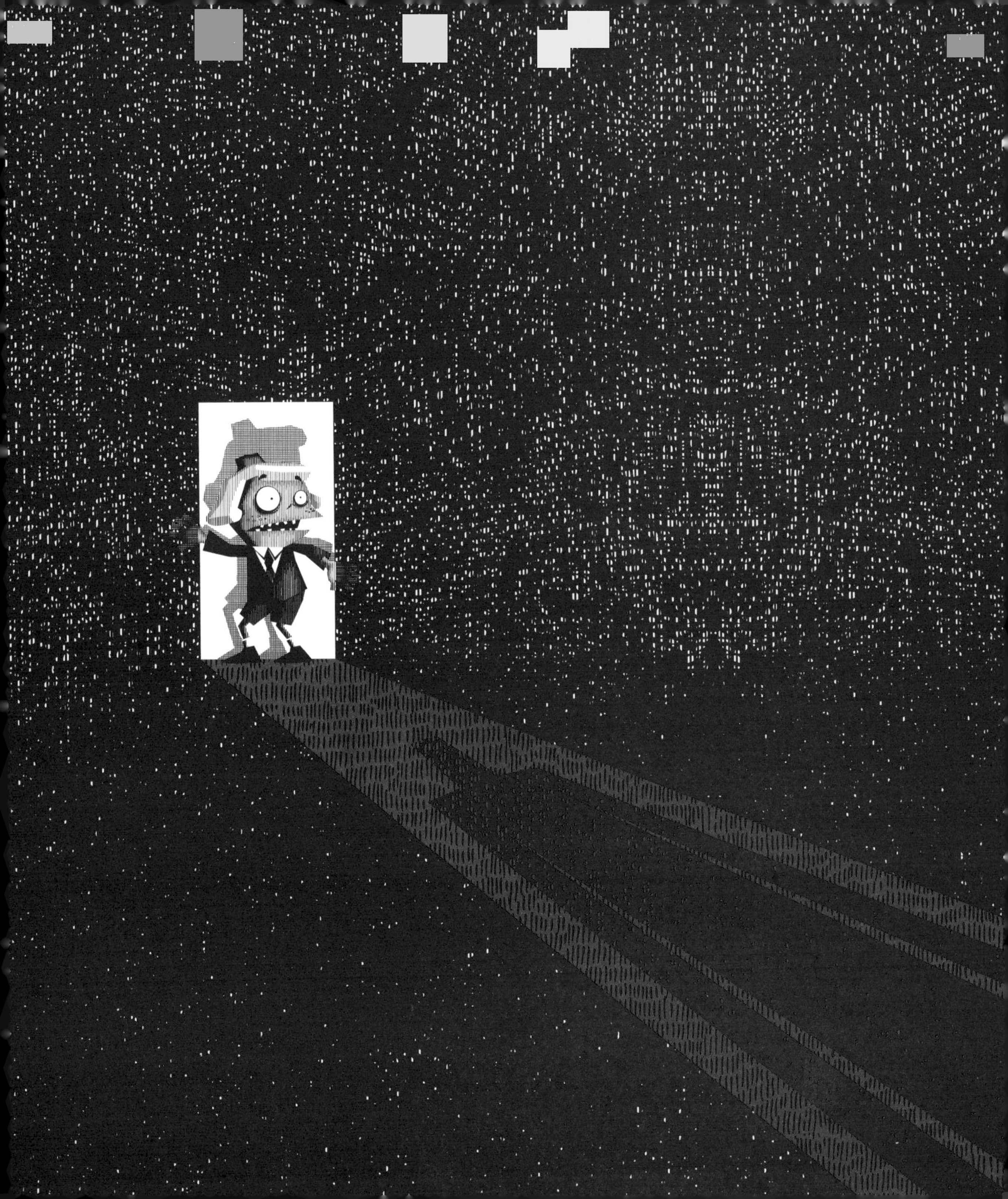

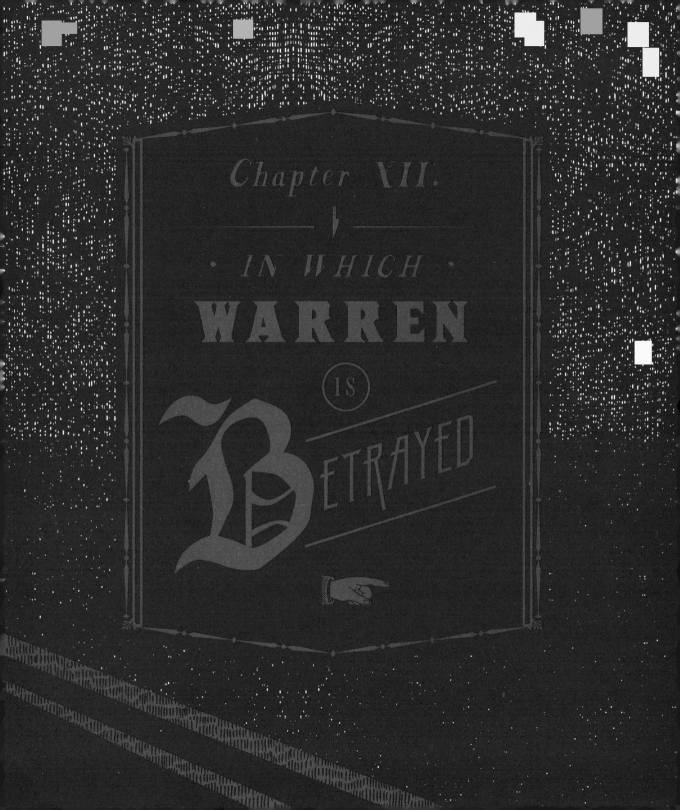

Chapter XII.

IN WHICH

WARREN

IS

Betrayed

 fter hours of tossing and turning, Warren finally managed to sleep, but his dreams were dark and muddled with visions of pirates, tidal waves, and snails in purple shells.

He awoke as the sun was beginning to rise; tiny beams of light leaked through the cracks in the attic walls. Warren let his eyes roam over the sketches he'd taped to his bedroom walls. He used to be able to draw trees and clocks and frogs and any other things that took his fancy. Now his sketchbook was bursting with a log of hotel repairs, and he had a cruel and vicious aunt who was up to no good. Warren wondered if he would ever have time to draw anything fun again.

Warren got dressed and brushed his yellow teeth. He was looking in the mirror combing his golden curls when he noticed something curious reflected in the glass. Three cards, facedown, had been slipped through the crack of his trap door.

Warren went to investigate. He instantly recognized the backs of the cards; they were from the same deck that Paleface carried. So he was still in the hotel after all!

Warren picked up the cards and turned them over one at a time. The first one showed a pair of dentures; the second one depicted a cane. Warren immediately thought of his tutor, Mr. Friggs. Then he turned over the third card and gasped. It was illustrated with an engraving of the journal!

Warren was so surprised, he nearly dropped the cards. What was Paleface trying to tell him? Was it possible that Mr. Friggs had somehow stolen the journal?

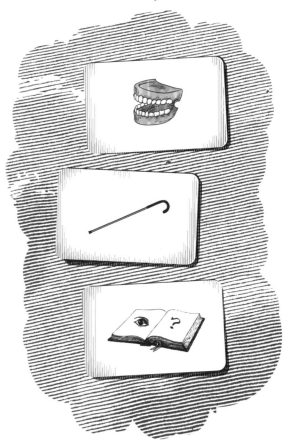

Was Mr. Friggs after the All-Seeing Eye, too?

Warren's stomach churned. He refused to jump to conclusions. He needed to talk things over with Petula, but he realized he didn't know her room number. Come to think of it, he'd never met her mother, either.

Warren headed downstairs and searched the dining hall, but there was no sign of his friend anywhere. He went to the kitchen and found Chef Bunion stirring an enormous pot of porridge. "It's going to be boiled oats for every meal until these guests learn to appreciate my cuisine!" He paused to reach into a jar. "You, on the other hand, get a giant pudding cookie."

Warren smiled and accepted the treat. "Thanks, Chef. I wish I could stick around and help, but something important has come up. Do you think you can manage on your own?"

"No problem, my boy! I'll just carry the pot out and let the guests serve themselves. See how they like that!"

"Great, Chef. Thank you." Warren turned to leave but then a thought occurred to him. "Oh, one more thing," he said. "Remember when I asked you about the old book? You said a man wearing bandages was reading it?"

"Of course I remember," Chef said. "It was only yesterday!"

"Do you remember what the book looked like?"

Chef shook his head. "I was too busy staring at the reader. He was really quite strange. As for the book, I didn't even notice the title. It was just a big red leather-bound book. Why do you ask?"

"No reason," Warren said, and he turned and walked away. The missing journal was small and blue, not big and red. Paleface never had it in the first place!

Warren left the kitchen and searched for Petula in all the common areas. He peeked into the lobby, the sewing room, the grand ballroom, and the game room, all to no avail. He even went down to the boiler room, but there was no sign of her [or Sketchy, for that matter]. Finally, Warren went out to the hedge maze. As he threaded through the passages, he lamented all the broken branches and crushed leaves left behind by careless guests. He didn't hear any screeches or chattering from the wild-life that usually called the shrubs home. Warren imagined they had all fled in terror.

Maybe they would never return.

When he reached the center of the maze, Warren was surprised to see Petula sitting serenely on the bench in front of the fountain. Surrounded by morning fog, she looked even more ghostly than usual, save the dark circles under her eyes. She must not have slept well, either.

"There you are," Warren said. "I've been looking for you!"

"I had to get out of the hotel," she replied. "It's all just too much."

"I have something to show you." He reached into his jacket pocket and pulled out the cards. "I think Paleface slipped these into my room last night."

Petula furrowed her brow. "I don't understand. What do they mean?"

"I think Paleface is trying to tell me that Mr. Friggs has the journal!"

"Your tutor?" Petula straightened. "Are you sure?"

"Well, Mr. Friggs uses a cane and has false teeth. Who else could it be?"

"But why would Mr. Friggs keep the journal from you? Wasn't he trying to help you find it?"

"He *said* he was," Warren said. "Only now I'm not so sure. I think we should go to the library and ask him."

Petula flashed Warren a curious look, her clear blue eyes sparkling with intensity. "Oh, we will," she said, but her voice sounded strange and hollow. Warren felt a prickle at the nape of his neck, a sensation that something was very wrong. Petula hopped off the bench and waved a hand in front of her face; in an instant, she was wearing a dark robe that concealed her face. Warren's mouth dropped open, but he made no sound except for a startled croak.

Warren tried to pull away, but Petula reached for his arm. With her other hand, she twirled a finger through the air, opening a portal. Petula stepped through the shimmering opening and pulled Warren after

her. His stomach turned as the world buckled and warped around him like a fun-house mirror.

The next thing he knew, they were standing in Aunt Annaconda's room. The Triangle Coven was lying in wait, their predatory smiles consuming their faces.

"Look who it is!" Annaconda said, clasping her hands. "My young apprentice. And she has brought my dear nephew along as well!"

Warren was aghast. He turned to Petula, but her face was hidden beneath her black cowl and she refused to meet his eyes. Warren's heartbreak was intense—almost as sharp as when his father died. He truly believed Petula was his friend. But he had been taken for a fool.

"Why?" he asked her softly.

Petula bowed to Annaconda. "We've located the journal."

Annaconda shrieked with delight. "Excellent! At last!" She whirled to face her sisters. "You've been surpassed by a little girl! She'll make a most powerful ally when I retrieve the All-Seeing Eye!"

Isosceles and Scalene did not share their sister's enthusiasm. Scalene glared at Petula with a murderous look, and Isosceles stuck out her tongue like a spoiled child.

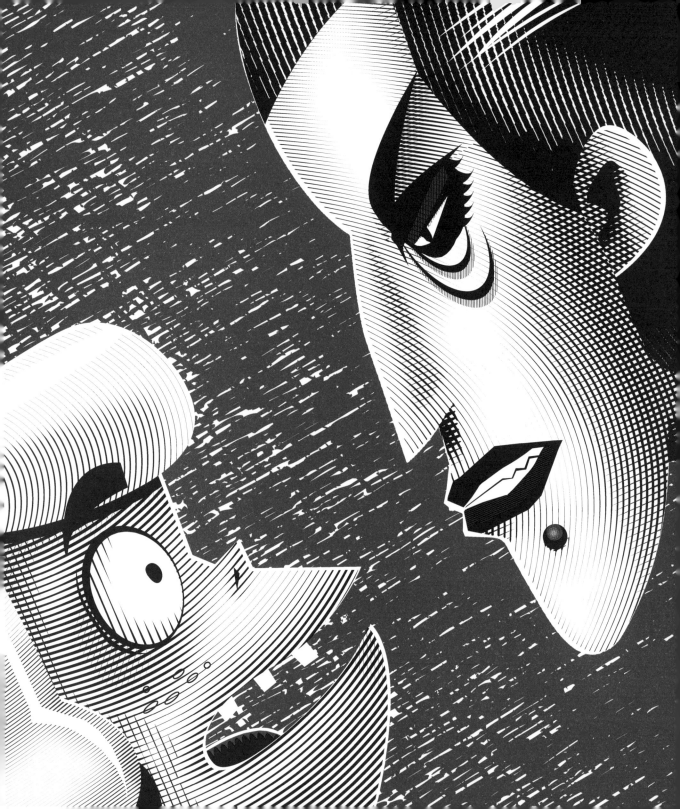

"Where is it?" Annaconda said to Warren. "Give it to me now!"

"I don't have it," Warren said, fighting to steady his voice.

"Then show me where it is!"

It was the first time Warren had ever refused his aunt—and he'd shouted the word "No!" at the top of his lungs. It felt tremendous! After four months of eating porridge and sleeping in the attic, after four months of suffering through her cruel and unusual punishments, Warren just couldn't take it anymore.

Annaconda's eyes widened and her bony hands tensed into claws. "What did you say?" Her face was white with fury, and Warren realized he was seeing a whole new side of his aunt, a side bordering on insanity.

Trills of terror ran down his spine, but he forced himself to stand tall. He wouldn't back down, no matter what. "You heard me the first time," he said, raising his voice. "I said *no*. I am not going to help. You may have tricked Uncle Rupert into getting married, but you haven't fooled me. You'll never find the All-Seeing Eye, not if I can help it!"

Warren knew he was being reckless. He knew Annaconda would punish him worse than she had ever punished him before. At any moment she was going to transform into a hideous snake, wrap her coils around his waist, and squeeze the life out of him.

But Petula intervened, cutting short the conversation. "Mr. Friggs has it," she said. "And that's not the only thing. We discovered that the All-Seeing Eye is hidden in a secret room. I think Mr. Friggs is guarding the entrance."

"Of course!" said Annaconda, stroking her chin thoughtfully. "I always wondered why the old fool spent all his time in the library. He's been sitting on the Eye the whole time. But today we take it back!"

Chapter XIII.

I

· IN WHICH ·

MR. FRIGGS

IS

MENACED

arren turned to run but Scalene and Isosceles grabbed his arms. Annaconda kicked open the door. "Let's go," she ordered.

The sisters proceeded to drag Warren across the hallway and down the stairs. "Uncle Rupert!" Warren yelled. "Chef Bunion! Somebody! Anybody! HELP!"

"Shut him up!" Annaconda snapped, and Scalene clamped a sweaty hand over Warren's mouth. Her palm smelled like moldy cheese and he chomped on it with his teeth. She yowled in pain.

"You wretched little brat!" she said, shaking her hand.

"Silence!" Annaconda shouted. "Do you want to attract the attention of every person in this hotel?"

Where were all the guests when you needed them? Warren realized with frustration that they were still finishing breakfast in the dining hall, too far away to hear his cries. His only hope was to appeal to the one person he believed was his friend. Petula was following closely on Annaconda's heels, her head bowed under her hood.

"Why would you do this?" Warren whispered to her. "You were being so nice. I thought you really liked me."

The girl's shoulders stiffened, but she said nothing.

They reached the library and found it locked. Annaconda pounded a bony fist against the thick oak door. "Open up!"

"Go away!" came Mr. Friggs's muffled reply. "I've had enough of people destroying my library!"

Annaconda nodded to Petula, and the apprentice stepped forward and drew a portal onto the door. It wavered eerily, like the rippling reflection on a pool of water. Petula and Annaconda stepped through first, followed by Scalene and Isosceles, tugging Warren after them. He felt another sickening wave of disorientation as he passed through.

They arrived to find Mr. Friggs waiting behind a barricade of the library's thickest almanacs and heaviest encyclopedias. He was dressed in his old military uniform and battle helmet, but he still needed his cane to stand up. With a wave of her hand, Annaconda knocked his books aside like toy blocks, scattering them to the floor.

"Where is the journal?" Annaconda demanded.

"I won't hand it over!" Mr. Friggs cried. "I've been entrusted to guard the hotel's secrets! And that's how it shall remain!"

Annaconda and Warren said at the same time.

"I'm sorry, Warren," said Mr. Friggs. "I've been concealing things for your own good. Your ancestors never wanted the

All-Seeing Eye to be found. All twelve generations have kept its location a secret."

Warren thought of the portraits in the Hall of Ancestors. "But if all the other Warrens knew, why didn't anyone tell me?"

"Your father was waiting until your eighteenth birthday, but he died before he could explain things to you—or to me. He had to keep the secret. He couldn't risk letting the Eye fall into the wrong hands. It's simply too powerful!"

Annaconda took hold of Mr. Friggs's shoulders and shook him like a rag doll. "Listen to me, you doddering fool! You don't need to tell Warren anything—but you must tell *me*! What is the All-Seeing Eye? Where is it? I need answers!"

"I don't know its location," Mr. Friggs insisted. "I only know that it is a kind of weapon. Constructed to protect and aid Warren the 1st through many battles. But once the wars were over, the Eye was hidden away so that no one would abuse it. That's why—"

"Enough with the history lesson!" Annaconda interrupted. "Just give me the journal! I'll figure out the rest for myself."

Mr. Friggs shook his head. "It belongs to Warren! It's his birthright!"

Petula turned to Annaconda with a

devilish grin. "Use the tooth, Your Darkness! Cast a spell on this foolish man and make him turn over the book!"

Annaconda removed the tooth from her pocket and held it before Mr. Friggs, who cowered at the sight of it. "I see you're familiar with my Malwoodian manticore tooth. Surely, then, you are aware of its extraordinary powers! Do I need to summon my last spell, or will you obey me willingly?"

"Use the magic, Your Darkness!" Petula exclaimed. "Take no chances!"

The color drained from Mr. Friggs's face. "Do your worst, you vile witch," he said. "I'm too old and tired to fight anymore."

Annaconda grabbed him by the arm, raising the tooth over her head—and for a moment Warren thought his teacher was truly doomed. But then the journal fell from inside his coat. Annaconda sprang forward, snatching it up greedily.

"At last!" she exclaimed. "And I didn't even need to waste my last spell!" She threw her head back and let out a joyful cackle. Scalene and Isosceles released Warren from their iron grip and joined their sister's

celebrations, dancing and cheering around Annaconda. Warren rubbed his arms and looked over at Petula. She wasn't celebrating. Instead, she stood silent and stiff, her hooded face a mystery.

"Thank you for your help, Mr. Friggs," Annaconda declared. "Now Scalene will see to it that you never trouble us again. Finish him off!"

"No!" Warren cried, rushing to his mentor's side. "He gave you what you wanted! Now leave him alone!"

"Shut up or you'll join him!" Annaconda barked. "Go on, Scalene. Get it over with."

Scalene licked her lips and rubbed her hands as she prowled toward Mr. Friggs. Warren could feel the old man tremble.

"I'd get out of the way, boy," Scalene warned. "After I change into a wolf I'll be very hungry, and you'll look like a tasty appetizer."

Warren refused to budge. "I hope you choke!"

Scalene raised her hands and began her transformation. A burst of purple light filled the room, along with the nauseating stink of sulfur.

What happened next took place so quickly, Warren could hardly believe his eyes: a figure leapt out from behind a bookshelf and uncorked a tiny bottle. It was Paleface! Then there was a loud *WHOOSH*, and the purple light seemed to be shrinking Scalene!

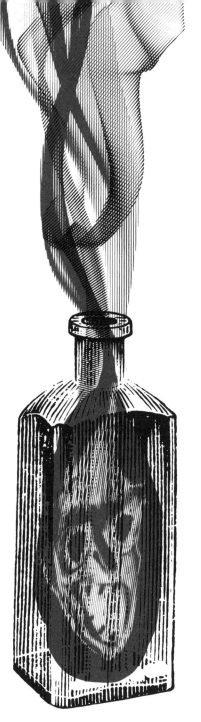

y
w

"Nooooo!" she screamed, her voice becoming tinny and faint. Her body stretched like taffy as the force pulled her inside the bottle. When Scalene was completely contained, Paleface popped in the cork and dropped the bottle in the red satchel, where it tinkled among dozens of similar vessels.

"A perfumier!" Annaconda gasped.

Petula ran to Paleface. "Way to go, Mom!"

"Mom?" Warren said.

Paleface reached and peeled back the bandages. That's when Warren realized that Paleface wasn't a he. She was a *she*! Petula's mother had the high sculpted cheekbones of a lady, and her face and neck were covered in tiny rose tattoos—the markings of a perfumier! She'd been working undercover all along!

Annaconda pointed at Petula accusingly. "So *that's* why you wanted me to use my magic! So your perfumier mother could capture me! Traitor!"

"I was never on your side to begin with!" Petula spat. She turned to Warren. "I wasn't double-crossing you! I was triple-crossing her!"

Warren was so confused, he didn't know what to say. He just hoped there was no such thing as a quadruple-cross. He wasn't sure he could trust anyone anymore!

Mr. Friggs turned to Warren and apologized, too. "I'm sorry I had to mislead you, my lad. But when you told me that a mysterious bandaged stranger had arrived, I knew immediately that it could mean only one thing: a perfumier in disguise. I searched the hotel until I found her sniffing around the hallway, and then I offered Beatrice my help."

"Beatrice?" Warren asked.

"That's my mother's real name," Petula explained. "My first night here, when I followed you into the hedge maze, she came with me. She was the one who took the journal, and then she gave it to Mr. Friggs so we could set a trap. We needed you to figure it out on your own, so you could lead Annaconda into it."

"How very clever!" Annaconda said with a sneer. "But all you've really managed to do is make me angry!" With a violent shove she pushed Isosceles into Beatrice, nearly knocking them both to the floor. Isosceles reached for the satchel as Beatrice struggled to protect it. "Release my sister!" Isosceles screamed. "Scalene, I'm going to free you! Hang on!"

Warren and Petula stepped forward to restrain Isosceles, and even Mr. Friggs tried to help by striking the witch with his cane. Isosceles seemed to realize she was overpowered and outnumbered; she rose to run but immediately tripped over an old dictionary and landed on the floor with a thud. With a blinding burst of purple light, Isosceles transformed into a vulture.

Beatrice reached for one of her bottles but wasn't fast enough. By the time she uncorked it, Isosceles was rising off the ground and flapping her wings, straining against the bottle's force. The perfumier's energy drew her closer and closer, twisting her downward like a vortex.

"You've almost got her!" Warren cried.

Isosceles struck Beatrice with a wing, breaking her concentration. Released from the force, she shot up like a rocket, bursting through the library's skylight with a *CRASH!* Through a rainstorm of glass, Beatrice bravely thrust out a hand and cast a quick spell. The shards immediately transformed into bits of paper that fluttered harmlessly to the floor. One of the scraps landed on Warren's shoulder, gentle as a leaf.

Petula ran to the window, but it was too late. Isosceles had escaped, soaring ever higher. "We failed," she said. "She got away."

Warren looked around and realized that Isosceles wasn't the only one who got away. Annaconda had vanished—and she'd taken the journal!

He turned to Beatrice. "Is there anything in the diary that I should know? Any hints that would help us find the All-Seeing Eye?"

Beatrice produced another card from

her deck—*fwip!* It was blank. Warren took this to mean: absolutely nothing.

"Mom's voice was stolen by a dark witch," Petula explained. "We've traveled the world trying to get it back."

"Are you sure the journal says nothing at all?" Warren asked again.

Petula shook her head. "It was pretty boring. I didn't see anything interesting."

"Then you didn't read it very carefully!" Mr. Friggs exclaimed. "One page in particular was unlike the others. I believe it contained a clue."

"What did it say?" Warren asked.

Mr. Friggs grinned shrewdly. "I can't tell you," he said, "but I can show you." He hobbled over and reached into an empty fish tank. He plucked out a page of the journal, shaking off the colorful gravel. "Fortunately, I had the presence of mind to keep it!"

Beatrice and Petula peered over Warren's shoulder. He was studying the page, wondering why it contained engravings of two little creatures: a rabbit and a snail.

ACTIVATION KEY:

ITS HOME IS A   ITS HOME

T H E
___ ___ ___   ___ ___ ___ ___ ___ ___   ___ ___ ___ ___ ___

"What's an activation key?" Warren asked.

"I'm not sure," said Mr. Friggs. "It appears to be some kind of riddle, but I was unable to unravel its meaning."

Warren continued examining the page. He loved word games. His father used to do a crossword every morning, and Warren learned a lot by watching him solve puzzles over breakfast. "A rabbit lives in a burrow," he said. "That's six letters long. It fits."

"And the second answer is easy," Petula chimed in. "A snail's home is a shell."

"The Burrow Shell!" Warren announced with satisfaction, though he was dismayed to realize the passcode didn't make a whole lot of sense. "The Burrow Shell?"

"Perhaps the Eye is hidden inside a burrow," Mr. Friggs offered.

"Or it's hidden in a shell inside a burrow," Petula suggested.

"Neither of those seems right," Warren said.

Beatrice reached into her cloak and pulled out two more cards—*fwip! fwip!* The first showed a clock face with bird wings; the second showed a fairy-tale witch wearing a pointy hat.

"Time flies! We need to find Anna-conda," Petula translated. "She still has one more spell and the ability to turn into her spirit animal. We need to find her before it's too late!"

"Good idea," Warren said. "But where should we look? She could be anywhere!"

nnaconda crouched on the floor of her sisters' room, flipping madly through the journal. Gripping a small mirror, she scanned the reflected pages as rapidly as possible. Her eyes darted left to right as she mumbled through the dated entries. "'Today I had the good fortune of eating a splendid tomato bisque soup, and while I do appreciate a good cracker, I may have added too many on this occasion, for they soaked up the broth like . . . ' WHAT IS THIS GARBAGE?!" she howled, her bony fingers shredding the paper.

Every page was filled with the same dull nonsense: endless entries about Warren Jr.'s daily activities. There were transcriptions of conversations and observations alongside anatomical diagrams of insects and arachnids in motion: spiders, scorpions, beetles, grasshoppers. Annaconda was tempted to fling the book out the window, but she was certain the words must have some meaning—she had to be missing a vital clue.

Outside her room, the distant chatter of guests returning from breakfast grew louder. Annaconda knew she didn't have much time. Soon everyone would resume searching for the All-Seeing Eye. And she couldn't hide much longer, not with Warren and that blasted perfumier on the loose. She had to stay on the move if she hoped to avoid them.

As Annaconda hurried into the hallway, she continued tearing out pages she deemed worthless, the scraps flittering like confetti in her wake. "More sketches of bugs!" she exclaimed. "Why was this idiot obsessed with bugs?"

"Hey, now, what's this?" said a woman's voice behind her. Annaconda whirled and saw the married acrobats in their sparkly bodysuits. They held a few of the torn pages and were studying them closely. "These look like clues," the man said.

The door to Room 804 flung open. "Clues? What clues?" said the gentleman jeweler.

Annaconda stomped over and snatched back the scraps. "Those are mine!"

"Finders keepers!" said the wife.

"It's a whole trail of clues!" the jeweler exclaimed, snatching ragged pages from the hallway floor.

The commotion was attracting attention. The door to Room 806 opened and then 807, 808, 809 . . . soon doors were opening all along the hallway. The hunchbacked woman thrust a gnarled finger at Annaconda. "She has a whole book of clues! Give us a look!"

Annaconda clutched the journal to her chest. "Be gone! All of you!"

Instead, even more guests streamed out, vying for a closer look at the journal. Annaconda ran to the main stairwell and

stumbled down the steps, hoping to find refuge in the basement. But upon reaching the third floor, she was met by even more guests coming in the other direction. News was spreading like wildfire!

"I don't have any clues!" she said anxiously. "This journal is worthless!"

"Then let us see it!" the barbarian shouted.

"Yes, give us a look," said the burly man in the safari outfit, "or my boy will fire his pop gun at you!"

Other angry voices joined the protest and the crowd circled around Annaconda. Matters were becoming desperate. Reaching into her pocket, she pulled out the tooth. "Don't make me use this!" she shouted.

> "I have powers you can't possibly comprehend!"

The guests drew back in awe—they thought it was another clue—and then swarmed around her, pushing and tugging. One grabbed for the journal while another lunged for the tooth. The boy with the pop gun shoved her from behind. "Final warning!" he threatened.

Annaconda knew she had no choice: she must resort to magic or lose everything forever. She scanned the hallway, making sure the perfumier was nowhere in sight, and then uttered the words to her final spell.

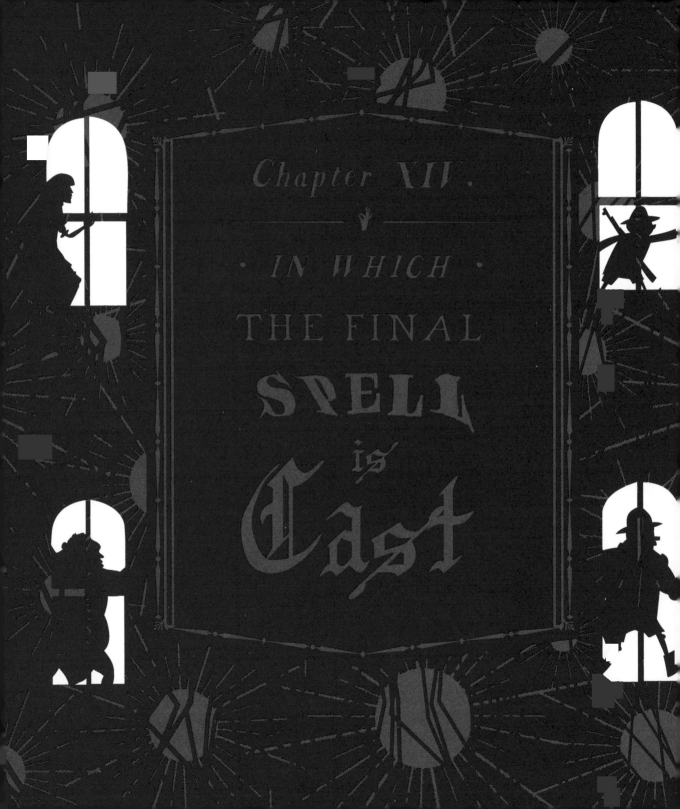

Chapter XIV.

· IN WHICH ·

THE FINAL

SPELL

is

Cast

ith the help of Beatrice's extraordinary sense of smell, Warren and his friends tracked Annaconda to the eighth floor. But by the time they reached the room of Isosceles and Scalene, Annaconda was gone. Beatrice prowled every corner, sniffing high and low. Petula followed close behind. Warren stood off to the side and tried to ignore the creepy objects cluttering the shelves and dressers; Annaconda's sisters had brought all kinds of strange possessions in their luggage.

There were eerie jars and vials and stacks of books that appeared to be bound in skin. Suspended from the ceiling was a string of dried bats; below them sat a cauldron from which tendrils of smoke coiled upward. Standing on his toes, Warren peered into the vessel, which looked to be bottomless. Curious, he reached inside.

"I wouldn't do that if I were you," Mr. Friggs said, using his cane to pull Warren back.

Beatrice flashed a series of cards—*fwip! fwip! fwip! fwip!*—and Petula translated for her: "Annaconda's scent is still strong. She can't be far away."

They left the bedroom, Beatrice sniffing wildly as they followed the trail down the hallway; Warren, Petula, and Mr. Friggs trailed along behind. Beatrice kept nodding and sniffing, past a tarnished statue of a weeping elephant and an antique writing desk stuffed with broken pencils, until they reached the stairwell.

"We're on the right track," Petula said.

When they reached the fourth-floor landing, they heard footsteps scampering up the stairs. Warren and the others pressed together in a protective knot as the sound grew louder and was accompanied by frantic panting and wheezing. The source of the noise finally appeared—it was Rupert! His face glowed red and rivulets of sweat coursed over his plump cheeks.

"Warren!" he gasped. "There you are! I've been looking all over!"

"Are you okay?" Warren asked.

"No! Come quick! There's an emergency!"

"What is it?" Warren asked.

"The hot water in my bathtub isn't working!"

"Your hot water?" Warren said. *"That's* your emergency?"

"But it's not hot at all," replied Rupert. "That's what I'm trying to explain. It's really rather tepid! Lukewarm! How am I supposed to bathe?"

"I have bigger problems right now, Uncle Rupert," Warren said. "Have you seen Aunt Annaconda?"

Rupert shook his head. "And I certainly do not want to see her, not until I've had my bath. I feel absolutely beastly!"

How could Uncle Rupert be so concerned about his bath at a time like this? In the stunned quiet that followed, Warren heard a commotion coming from the lower floors. The din from a mass of voices was followed by Annaconda's high-pitched shriek. Suddenly, a flash of purple light appeared, followed by silence.

Beatrice was already racing down the stairs. Warren and Petula darted after her, with slow-moving Mr. Friggs and an exasperated Rupert lagging behind. "Will you need any plumbing tools?" he asked. "I believe there is a wrench under the reception desk—"

Warren hurried along. On the third-floor landing, the air was still thick with the putrid scent of sulfur. "We're too late!" Petula cried. "She used the tooth!"

Limp bodies were strewn the length of the hallway, and Warren felt a sickening rush of horror. Were they dead? Then he heard the soft sound of restful breathing rippling through the air.

Rupert wandered among the guests. "Whasssgoin' on?" he said. "Whyss everybody lying down?" Then his eyes rolled back and he slumped to his knees. With a *thud*, he toppled to the floor, his loud snuffles joining the chorus of snores.

"A sleep spell," Mr. Friggs said weakly, leaning heavily on his cane. "She's cursed the entire hotel!"

Warren was feeling quite sleepy, indeed. He blinked heavily and glanced at Petula; she too had a dazed expression. Despite an unsteady wobble, Beatrice was hunting through the folds of her cloak. Warren felt his eyelids starting to droop; his vision blurred. If he could just take a quick little nap . . .

Warren was vaguely aware of Beatrice waving something in the air. It was a stone from which emanated a dome of blue light, encasing him and his friends within it. Almost instantly, the fog in Warren's brain lifted and he felt more alert.

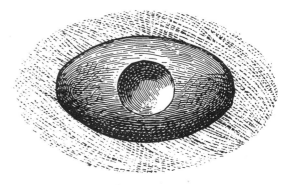

"Phew!" Petula said. "That was a close one."

Beatrice nodded grimly and tucked the stone inside her cloak.

"What happened?" Warren asked.

"Thanks to Mom, we're protected from the effects of your aunt's spell," Petula explained. "We'll see about reviving the guests later, but first we better find Annaconda!"

"She's used her last spell," said Mr. Friggs. "She might be closer to the Eye than we thought! There must be something in the journal that I overlooked."

"She knows the hotel has a hidden room," Warren reminded him. "Maybe she's looking for the Heart of the Warren."

"Perhaps," Mr. Friggs said, stroking his sideburns. "That would be the next logical step."

They rushed to the library, but it was too late. Annaconda had been there not moments earlier, searching for secret doorways or a hidden passage in the floor. "My precious books!" Mr. Friggs wailed, stooping to gently pick up a ripped volume as if it was baby bird with broken wings. Entire bookshelves had been toppled, their contents tossed recklessly on the floor.

"This isn't the Heart of the Warren, it's the Brain of the Warren," said Petula. "Where would she look next?"

Warren wracked his brain. "The lobby?"

Down they all went to the first floor, though Annaconda wasn't there either. But she had been. Rupert's desk was flipped on its side and the curtains ripped clean off their rods.

"We're always two steps behind her," Mr. Friggs said. "We'll only catch her if we anticipate where she'll look next."

Everyone turned to Warren. A mixture of pressure and pride swelled inside his chest—he knew the building better than anyone else, had spent his childhood exploring every cranny and corner. Where could the Heart of the Warren be?

" THE "
KITCHEN!

he announced. "That *must* be the Heart of the Warren!"

Mr. Friggs nodded. "Home is where the hearth is!"

"Brilliant!" said Petula. "Let's go!"

The group hurried down to the basement. As they approached the kitchen, they could hear the clatter of shattering glass and pots and pans being thrown across the room. "Careful, now," warned Mr. Friggs in hushed tones. They huddled together and pushed open the doors.

A frenzied Annaconda was tearing through the cabinets in a rage. Warren was relieved to find Chef Bunion safely asleep; he was sprawled on a countertop, his head resting on a bread loaf like a pillow. Warren could only imagine how angry he'd be to witness Annaconda's rampage through his cherished kitchen.

Having destroyed one wall of cupboards, Annaconda spun around and came face to face with Warren and his friends. "How can this be?" she screamed. "You should be asleep like the rest!"

"My mom is a powerful witch, remember?" Petula said. "Your last spell was a waste!"

Annaconda roared in frustration. She grabbed a huge iron skillet and flung it at their heads. Everyone ducked except poor Mr. Friggs; the handle of the pan clipped his cane and sent him cascading to the floor.

Warren knew he had to act fast. Annaconda's violence knew no bounds.

"Oh, Auntie," he sang in his sweetest voice. "There's one page you haven't seen yet. Mr. Friggs had it hidden in his fish tank. I believe it contains some very important information."

He reached into his jacket and pulled out the paper with the engraving of the rabbit and the snail.

"Give that to me!" Annaconda demanded, lunging toward him. Her reflexes were quick, but Warren was quicker. He jumped aside and scurried to the sink, jamming the page into the drain. His hand was tiny enough to reach far down into the pipe, where he knew Annaconda's would never fit.

Annaconda shoved Warren aside and tried to plunge her hand into the drain, but only three of her fingers would fit. She shrieked again in frustration.

"I guess there's no way of getting it now," Warren said.

But there was a way. He knew it, and so did his aunt Annaconda: If she changed into a snake, she could easily slither down the pipe. And then Beatrice could imprison her during her transformation!

Annaconda's eyes flickered and in a low voice she said, "You must think I'm stupid! I'm not going to transform with a perfumier in the room!"

She knelt and began tugging at the pipe under the sink. "No need to use magic when force will do!"

"Then we'll use force, too!" Warren yelled, rushing forward. The others followed, and together they managed to overpower Annaconda and pry her hands off the pipe. She fought and screamed and flapped her arms as they dragged her over to the laundry room next to the kitchen, shoving her inside. Before the door slammed shut, Warren managed to wrest the journal out of her hands. Annaconda pummeled and scratched at the heavy bolted door, but all her efforts were in vain.

She was trapped.

"My journal!" she screamed. Another muffled screech sounded from the other side of the door. "Let me out!"

"Without magic, there's no way she can escape," said Petula. "We can deal with her later. Let's see the journal!"

The group huddled around Warren as he flipped through the pages. "I can't read it without a mirror," he said, so Petula handed him a shiny, brand-new skillet. He held it up to show the words reflected in its surface.

True to Mr. Friggs's description, all the entries seemed ordinary and dull. On any other occasion, Warren would have relished reading about the daily life of Warren the 2nd, but all he could think about now was finding another clue.

He tried hard to concentrate but was growing distracted. The pounding of Annaconda's fists was joined by a second worrisome sound: the low rumble of thunder. A storm was blowing in from the forest.

Warren shook off a chill. He continued

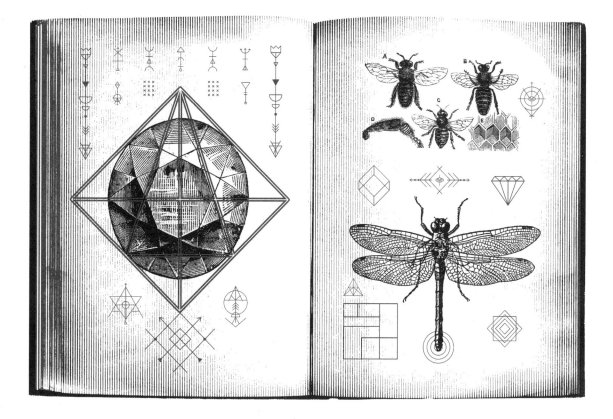

thumbing through the book, its pages covered with illustrations of insects, sometimes complete bugs and sometimes only their legs. "It's just weird doodles," he said, pointing to the insects' spindly limbs, their knees bent and feet flat. "I'm stumped."

"Me, too," said Mr. Friggs. "Between the poem and the puzzle and the map in the painting, I know we're so close. But I'm not sure we'll ever figure it out."

"At least we don't have to worry about Annaconda finding the Eye," Petula said. "She won't dare leave the laundry room with Mom guarding the door."

"But Isosceles is still on the loose," Warren said. "We can't stop searching. Otherwise she might find it before we do."

Another crack of thunder rattled Warren's thoughts. He closed his eyes and shivered, trying to shake off the icy cold invading the room. He summoned the words of the poem from memory:

"When the Heart of the Warren hears
the tone played by the rightful hand
The All—Seeing Eye will appear,
Granting dominion across the land.

And when the Heart of the Warren sees
The words writ by the rightful man.
The All—Seeing Eye commandeered,
The hotel shall no longer stand."

Warren knew *he* was the "rightful man"—as the thirteenth Warren, he had to be. But what was the Heart of the Warren? And, more important, *where* was it?

The radiator pipes rattled as warm water gurgled up from the boiler. The room had grown so cold that the hotel's heating system switched on. Warren was relieved—one less task he had to worry about.

And then it hit him:

"The Heart of the Warren!"

he exclaimed. "It's the place that pumps heat to the rest of the building, like a heart pumps blood!"

Everyone looked at him in awe.

"To the boiler room!" they cried.

Chapter XV.

IN WHICH

THE HEART OF THE

Warren

is

FOUND

eatrice stayed behind to guard the laundry room door while Warren, Mr. Friggs, and Petula headed to the boiler room. "Before we go inside," Warren said, "I need to warn you about something."

"What is it?" Petula asked.

"Well, it's kind of hard to explain," Warren said. "Maybe I better just show you."

Mr. Friggs and Petula exchanged nervous glances as Warren pushed open the door. Another crack of thunder shook the hotel, but the room felt cozy and warm, the small space dimly lit by the boiler's flame.

Mr. Friggs tapped his cane on the brick wall, searching for secret doors or hidden triggers. Petula peered about, confused. "What's the big secret?"

"It's a little shy," Warren said.

"What's a little shy?" Petula asked.

Warren jingled one of the service bells. As its clear tone echoed off the walls, Warren heard the familiar thumping and slurping. Like a happy puppy, Sketchy sprang out from behind the boiler, wriggling its tentacles and slithering across the floor.

Mr. Friggs shrieked and huddled close to Petula. Sketchy shrieked even louder and huddled close to Warren. Its many eyes studied the newcomers with trepidation.

"Okay, everybody calm down," Warren said. "Mr. Friggs and Petula, I'd like you

to meet Sketchy. I don't know if Sketchy is a he or a she or neither or both. But I do know that Sketchy is very friendly and likes art and cookies!"

Sketchy's response was not friendly at all. The creature whistled like an angry teakettle and then lurched toward Petula and Mr. Friggs, waving its tentacles aggressively.

Everything was going wrong! "No, Sketchy, these are my friends! *Friends*. Like you and me."

After a few tense seconds, Sketchy seemed to understand. It began whistling a happier tune and lowered its tentacles, using them to draw the three friends into a group hug. "Easy now!" Mr. Friggs wheezed, but

Sketchy squeezed until the man's dentures popped out. Then it released everyone and clapped its tentacles cheerfully.

"What *is* it?" Petula asked.

Mr. Friggs retrieved his dentures and popped them back in to his mouth. "I've never seen anything quite like it. I certainly don't know where it came from!"

"I think Sketchy's been here a long, long time," Warren said. "Remember that squiggly star shape on the blueprints? I think that's Sketchy. I think it was put here in the Heart of the Warren to guard the hotel's secret."

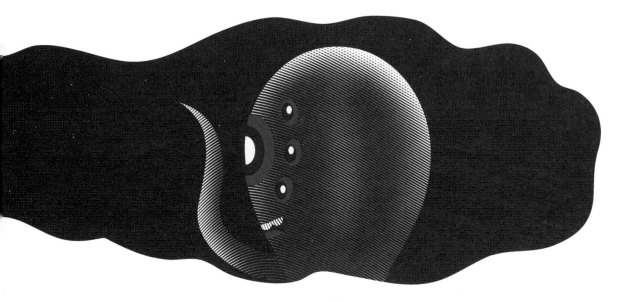

"But that means the secret room is on the other side of this wall!" Petula said. "How do we get to the All-Seeing Eye?"

At the mere mention of the All-Seeing Eye, Sketchy wiggled its tentacles and whistled a happy melody. Warren recognized the song. It was the same one Sketchy had sung to help Warren fall sleep.

"You know about the Eye!" he exclaimed. "What is it?"

Sketchy simply repeated the same melody, over and over.

Mr. Friggs shook his head. "It's a lovely tune," he said in frustration, "but I wish the creature would just talk to us!"

"It *is* talking," Petula said thoughtfully. "We just don't understand what it's trying to say."

Sketchy bobbed and swayed, whistling even louder. It was definitely some kind of language. Sketchy seemed to be saying: *Keep guessing! You've almost got it!*

"Is it the boiler?" Mr. Friggs asked. "Shall we rip out the boiler? Or crawl *inside* the boiler?"

Sketchy stopped whistling: *Try again.*

"Maybe we need to talk like Sketchy," Warren said.

He tried whistling the melody back to the creature. It recognized the tune and grew more animated, spinning in circles, tentacles waving excitedly. Sketchy warbled the melody again and again.

"It's working!" Petula said. "I don't know what it's trying to say, but it wants you to repeat that melody!"

Warren whistled the song a dozen times, until his lips were sore and his mouth hurt. Then Petula and Mr. Friggs took turns, but Sketchy just kept waving its tentacles, gesturing for more: *Keep going, you're almost there but you haven't quite got it.*

Warren glanced around anxiously. Then a slight movement caught his eye. It was the hotel snail, the one with the cracked purple shell, trailing along the wall next to the bells.

The bells!

"I've got it!" Warren exclaimed. "It's not the whistling. It's the tone. Just like the riddle says: 'When the Heart of the Warren hears the tone played by the rightful hand, the All-Seeing Eye will appear, granting dominion across the land!'" He reached up and tapped on the bells. It took a few tries, but eventually he copied the notes exactly.

Suddenly the entire boiler room started to shake. "This is the tone," Warren said, "and I'm the rightful hand!"

Amid the clamor of clanking gears and grinding machinery, the boiler hissed like an angry beast and vented plumes of hot steam. For a moment Warren was shrouded in thick fog. He couldn't see his friends—he couldn't see anything. But when the vapors finally settled, the boiler had shifted several feet, revealing a large oblong door.

The door's surface was painted to resemble a large blue eye, with its central doorknob colored black like a pupil. The effect was uncanny. Warren stared at the door, which seemed to be staring back.

"The secret room!" said Petula excitedly. "We found it!"

"I knew it!" Warren exclaimed.

Sketchy whistled happily. It extended a tentacle and gently nudged Warren toward the door. He gulped and looked at his friends, who nodded encouragingly. "All right, here goes. Wish me luck, everybody."

Warren reached to open the door but suddenly stopped short. Much to his astonishment, the hotel snail had crept down the wall and was now perched atop the knob! Warren had only a moment to marvel at the mollusk's speed when the snail began to laugh. It was low and sinister, a hideous cackle. Horror flooded Warren's veins as he realized the snail's true identity. Then the room filled with the sound of a thunderclap and a burst of purple light. There stood Aunt Annaconda!

"YOU'RE A SNAIL?"

Warren said in disbelief.

"That's right, you little dummy!"

"But your name is—I thought your spirit animal was—"

"A snake?" Annaconda interrupted. "Thank Darkness, I'm not! The mighty snail is a far superior creature. She travels in stealth and no one ever sees her coming. For the past four months, I've been following you around, spying on you and searching for clues. I had no trouble escaping down the laundry room drain in this form. Your stupid perfumier is still guarding the door like a dolt!"

Petula darted toward the exit but Annaconda grabbed her arm and twisted it backward. "Oh, no you don't!" she hissed. "You're not going anywhere, you little do-gooder!"

Petula cried out. Warren rushed to help but Sketchy slithered in front of him.

The creature used half its tentacles to pry Petula free and the other half to restrain Annaconda.

"Thattagirl!" Mr. Friggs cheered, waving his cane in the air. "I mean, thattamonster!"

"Release me!" Annaconda shrieked, straining to free herself from the tentacles' ever-tightening grip. But she was no match for Sketchy. "You see this?" she said, producing the engraving Warren had stuffed down the drain. "A snail! It's clearly a sign! The All-Seeing Eye is meant to be mine! So tell your little pet to let me go or else!"

"Or else what?" Warren said. "You have no magic left! You don't scare me!"

"Is that so?" said Annaconda, and a devious smile spread across her face. Thunder crashed outside and the boiler's flames flickered ominously. Then she pulled out the tooth and stabbed Sketchy in the tentacle. The monster whistled in surprise and collapsed, releasing its hold.

"Sketchy!" Warren cried, rushing to the monster. "Are you okay?"

Its many eyes were squeezed shut in agony, and it released a faint trill. Purplish liquid seeped from the wound. Warren stroked his friend softly as he choked back a sob. His wretched, evil aunt had already hurt Petula, and now poor Sketchy, too. Was Mr. Friggs next? Warren felt sick. This was all his fault.

"Enough!" he cried. "I'll do whatever you want. Just stop hurting my friends!"

"That's better," said Annaconda. "Now get up, all of you. I'm going through that door to the All-Seeing Eye, and you're coming with me in case it's a trap."

Petula rose to her feet, her injured left arm hanging awkwardly at her side. Mr. Friggs hobbled wearily to Annaconda. Warren could see the fight had left his friends, and fear settled over him. He stood on shaking limbs. Sketchy reached out a tentacle and coiled it around Warren's leg: *Don't go . . .*

"It's okay, Sketchy." Warren didn't want to leave his hurt friend, but he had no choice. He quickly loosened his tie and used it to bandage Sketchy's wound. The creature heaved slowly, whistling with each labored breath. "You rest here, buddy, and wait for me to come back. Everything is going to be all right."

"Hurry up!" Annaconda snapped. "Get in front of me! March!"

Warren stood up and plodded over as if his feet were made of lead. Annaconda shoved him toward the eye-shaped door.

"Open it."

Warren's hand trembled as he grasped the doorknob. Just moments ago he had felt such excitement. Now he felt only dread.

Chapter XVI.

· IN WHICH ·

The

FINAL

RIDDLE IS

SOLVED

lowly, Warren opened the door. A narrow tunnel stretched out in front of him, extending into complete darkness. He hesitated. "What are you waiting for?" Annaconda said, prodding him in the back. "Go on, you little troll! Move!"

Warren gulped and stepped forward, his hands out in front of him as he tried to sense the way. Smothered in obscurity, he stepped on something soft and stopped short, causing a chain reaction as the others bumped into him. Annaconda let out a curse and ordered Petula to use magic to light a torch.

"You sprained my casting arm," Petula said. "It hurts too much."

"I don't care how much it hurts!" Annaconda exclaimed. "Light up this tunnel or I'll sprain more than your arm!"

Petula whimpered as she cast the spell. Too weak to create more than a dim glow, she moved the flame in a circle, offering glimpses of their surroundings. "This is all the magic I can summon."

Warren looked down and realized that what he had stepped on was a length of hose. He saw that walls were lined with even more hoses as well as pipes and ropes, as if they had entered the belly of an enormous machine. The group pressed on, at last emerging into a small windowless room. Beside the entrance, there was a cluster of candles and Petula touched her finger to the wicks; they bloomed with light, casting a soft glow.

In the center of the room was a tall chair and a large mechanical panel cluttered with buttons and levers. It looked like the controls to a carnival ride.

"What is all this?" Warren wondered aloud.

"Some kind of operations console," Mr. Friggs said. "I must say, I'm rather impressed! Such a modern-looking device, and yet it was built by your forefathers hundreds of years ago. That's really quite—"

"Out of my way!" Annaconda snapped, shoving Warren and his friends aside and plopping into the chair. She clasped her hands gleefully. "The All-Seeing Eye must be locked behind these controls!"

She pounded her fists on the various buttons, but nothing happened.

"What is the meaning of this?" she cried. "It's not working!"

"I believe the terminal may be operated only by someone of the Warren lineage," Mr. Friggs said softly. "It's not meant for the likes of you."

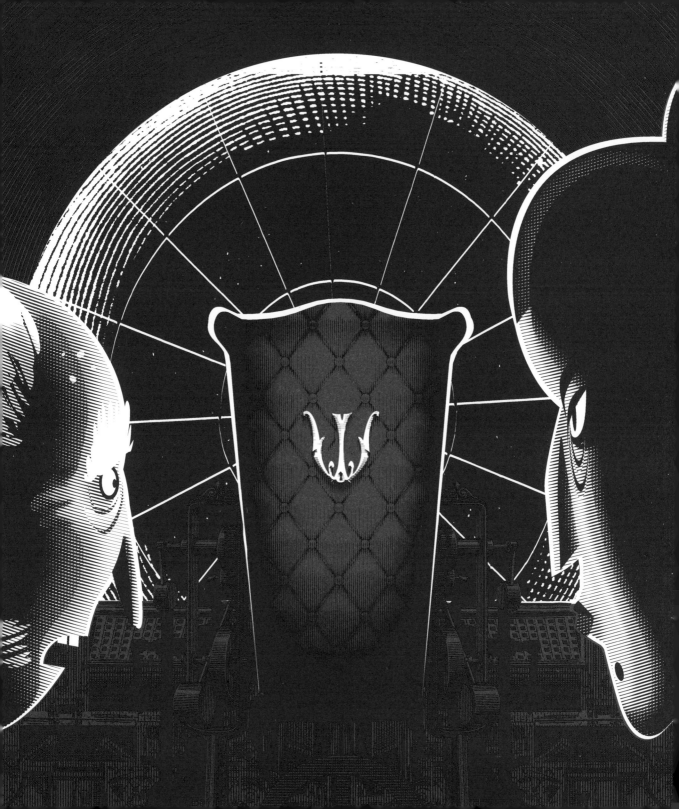

Annaconda shot him a murderous glare and then shifted her gaze to Warren. "Get in the chair, toadface!" she ordered. "Make it work. I'm so close to the All-Seeing Eye, I can *feel* it!"

She stuffed Warren into the seat. He looked at the controls, moving his hand over the square buttons, toggle switches, brass levers, and round dials. Nothing was labeled and he didn't know what to do. Which button should he press or what toggle should he pull? What if something bad happened?

Annaconda screeched.

Finally, Warren decided on a small panel ringed with tiny glass bulbs. He couldn't explain why he chose it—it just felt right. As soon as he touched the panel, the bulbs lit up and Warren felt a jolt of electricity run up his arm.

From somewhere below came a deep rumbling sound. One might have mistaken the noise for thunder, except the walls and the floor were trembling too, as if in an earthquake.

"Yes!" Annaconda hooted with delight. "Feel the power of the All-Seeing Eye!"

More lights blinked to life, flashing and filling the room with kaleidoscopic colors. Warren felt an odd, dizzying pressure in the pit of his stomach, just like when he would ride in the hotel's dumbwaiter at top speed. He felt as if he was rising up, up into the air.

Mr. Friggs dropped his cane and grasped Warren's chair to steady himself. "Careful, my dear boy! Don't touch anything else! You seem to have activated it!"

The room was shaking more violently than ever. Dust and plaster dropped from the ceiling. It felt as if the roof was about to collapse.

"Maybe we should leave," Petula said.

"Silence!" Annaconda shrieked. "No one moves! Not until I get what I came for!" She looked frantically around the control room until her eyes settled on a small hatch in the floor. A look of crazed glee crossed her face. She yanked on the handle and the hatch flew open. A cold wet wind blasted into the room. Mr. Friggs collided with Petula, and both of them toppled to the floor. Warren knelt down and peered down the hatch.

He couldn't believe his eyes!

A thunderstorm seemed to be raging *underneath* the basement of the hotel. It didn't make any sense. Warren quickly realized they were no longer on the ground. The hotel had been lifted eight or nine stories into the air. Warren could see the hotel's foundation, now nothing more than a large muddy pit. On the sides of the building, four tall mechanical pillars were anchored to the ground. They extended from the base like insect legs.

"I've found it!" Annaconda cried. "The Eye is buried *below* the hotel!"

She reached to open a small panel beside the hatch and a long rope ladder spilled out, unfurling and swaying madly in the thunderstorm. Annaconda grabbed the top rung and began her descent.

"The burrow," Petula said, remembering the riddle. "You have to *burrow* under the hotel to get to the Eye! Why didn't I think of that?"

"But then what's the shell?" Warren asked. A nagging thought kept tugging at the back of his mind. Something wasn't right. He was so puzzled that he almost didn't notice Petula crawling over to the hatch.

"Wait, where are you going?"

"We can't let Annaconda get the Eye," Petula said, grabbing the ladder's rungs.

"But your arm!" Warren yelled. "You can't climb!"

Petula explained, "As a perfumier-in-training, I've been waiting for this opportunity my whole life." She hooked her good arm through a rung to steady herself, then reached for a tiny bottle and showed it to Warren. "If she finds the Eye and her powers are restored, I need to be there to capture her."

The ladder swung wildly, like the pendulum of a grandfather clock. Anaconda was nearly at the bottom, oblivious to her pursuer. Petula lowered herself slowly, one rung at a time. As Warren watched, he noticed that the legs of the hotel were adorned with gears, cogs, and pistons. The entire building trembled precariously.

Back at the control panel, Mr. Friggs was using his cane to raise himself off the ground. "This is too dangerous, Warren. We need to stabilize the building. Try one of the other buttons."

"But which one?" Warren exclaimed.

There were too many, hundreds of them, all different shapes and sizes and colors. Warren pressed a round green button but nothing happened. Then he tugged a black lever that produced a faint hum but little else. Next he tried turning a black dial from 5 to 6, but the mechanism refused to budge.

"Don't give up," Mr. Friggs said. "There's clearly power flowing into this panel, but something is locking the controls. Perhaps we need a passcode."

"That's it!" Warren exclaimed. He turned to a grid of buttons that resembled a keypad. "Remember the journal page?

"THE ACTIVATION KEY?"

Mr. Friggs's mouth widened into a grin: "'When the Heart of the Warren sees the words writ by the rightful man.' Warren, my boy, that's it! Type in the code and let's see what happens!"

Warren tapped the letters one at a time: T-H-E B-U-R-R-O-W S-H-E-L-L.

An angry horn sounded and the hotel shuddered. Flakes of plaster rained down from the ceiling, and a large crack spread across the floor. A small slip of paper spooled out of a slot; Warren saw the word stamped on it in smudged ink:

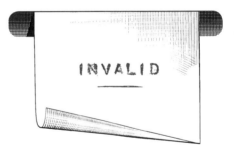

"Try something else!" said Mr. Friggs. "What else is there?" Warren asked. "Try anything! We're about to fall over!"

ACTIVATION KEY:

THE   *ITS HOME IS A*   *ITS HOME*

Warren tried his best to remember exactly how the page had looked.

Countless rabbits lived in the forest around the hotel, but Warren knew nothing about them. Their home was underground. They lived in burrows. They lived in shafts and passages and dirt, but none of those words fit the blanks. They lived in a—

"Warren!" Mr. Friggs shouted.

Warren looked at his tutor. "Yes?"

"No, my boy, that's the answer!" said Mr. Friggs. "Rabbits live in a warren!"

Of course! Warren couldn't believe he hadn't thought of it sooner. He rushed over to the typewriter-like device and typed:

T-H-E W-A-R-R-E-N S-H-E-L-L.

Once again, the hotel shuddered, an angry horn blared, and another paper stamped INVALID spooled from the slot and fluttered to Warren's feet. By now the crack in the floor had spread to all four walls, causing Mr. Friggs to glance around nervously. "We can't wait much longer," he said. "We may have only one more guess!"

The room teetered more violently than ever. It seemed as if the building were cracking apart. After trying so hard to save his family's hotel, Warren felt that he was destroying it single-handedly. A snail's home was hard. A snail's home was safe . . .

A chunk of falling plaster narrowly missed Warren's head. "Move!" Mr. Friggs shouted.

Warren ducked in the nick of time. "Exactly!" he said. "It moves!"

"I beg your pardon?"

"A snail's home moves!" Warren cried. "That fits the blanks!"

He leaned over the keypad and typed: T-H-E W-A-R-R-E-N M-O-V-E-S. In an instant, all the buttons on the console flashed bright green and a cheerful bell sounded. There was a loud clanking noise and a long metal tube descended from an opening in the ceiling. Attached to the end was a pair of goggles, fitted with a crank on one side and a lever on the other. They stopped directly in front of Warren's face. He looked into the lenses and gasped.

Through a series of cleverly placed mirrors, Warren could see *outside* the hotel. He saw the gloomy forest and the trees whipping in the thrashing rain.

Turning the crank adjusted the view, allowing Warren to see in different directions. He saw the hedge maze and the driveway winding through the woods. He was up so high, he could even see the next village miles and miles away.

"Mr. Friggs, it's a periscope!" Warren cried. "Like on a submarine! You control it with the crank."

"What about the lever?" Mr. Friggs asked.

Warren pushed the lever and the hotel lurched forward. Mr. Friggs was knocked off balance and spilled to the floor. He peeked into the hatch and then turned to Warren in astonishment. "The pillars are moving! The hotel is . . . *walking*!"

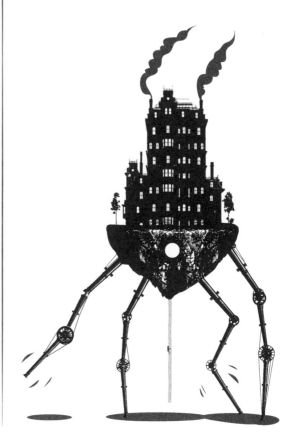

Warren could feel the structure rising and falling with each step. He released the lever but the building kept tromping and trudging across the lawns, heading for the forest. He looked down at the control panel and grabbed the round wheel; the hotel veered sharply to the right. It was walking in a circle. With every step forward, its enormous metal legs made a deafening

CLANG~CLANG~CLANG~CLANG!

A faint voice wafted up through the hatch. "Hellllllllllp!"

"Petula!" Warren cried.

He peered down and saw Petula clinging desperately to the ladder; she was swaying to and fro, hanging on for dear life. With one arm injured, she surely wouldn't last much

190

longer. They had to find some way to slow down!

"The girl is in danger!" Mr. Friggs shouted. "Warren, you need to stop this thing! Find the brake!"

Warren stared helplessly at the control panel. He pushed a big blue button and the hotel leapt into the air like a ballerina; it crashed down in the forest, splintering trees like tiny matchsticks. Warren tried more buttons—he tried every button—and the hotel did everything but stop. It pranced, it galloped, it hopped on two legs instead of four, it even skipped! Petula shrieked:

"WARRRRRRRREN!"

Mr. Friggs knelt beside the hatch and pulled on the ladder, but he wasn't strong enough.

Warren didn't want to leave the controls unattended, but he knew he had to help Mr. Friggs. He rushed over and together they managed to raise the ladder, one soaking wet rung at a time. Sweat broke out on Warren's brow and his muscles strained. But as they pulled Petula closer—and he saw the terror on her face—he found a strength he didn't know he had. At last she was able to grasp the edge of the hatch, and Warren pulled her up into the control room.

"What's happening?" she exclaimed. "Why is the hotel walking?"

"There's no time to explain," Warren said, and he ran back to the chair to look through the goggles. The hotel had marched in a wide circle through the forest, leaving behind a trail of destruction. Now it was heading back toward the foundation—a giant muddy pit!

"Do something!" shouted Mr. Friggs.

"I already tried all the buttons!" Warren said.

"Then try something else!" Mr. Friggs cried.

But it was too late. There were no brakes, so Warren cranked the wheel to the right in a last-ditch attempt to avoid the massive hole.

The room lurched to the left, and yet again Mr. Friggs was thrown off balance. The old man grabbed a cable from the ceiling, triggering a loud screech and a gnashing of gears. All at once, the clanking noises ceased. Steam hissed through the tubes as though releasing a long and beleaguered sigh. Finally the hotel stopped.

Warren smiled in relief as his friends rushed over and hugged him. "You did it, Warren!" Petula cried. "You figured it out!"

"With your help," he said.

Warren's tutor was so overjoyed, he looked ready to cry. "It's incredible!" he said. "'The All-Seeing Eye commandeered, the hotel shall no longer stand!' It all makes sense now! The hotel *is* the All-Seeing Eye and it no longer stands, it *walks*!"

Warren was amazed. Somehow all twelve of his ancestors had managed to keep this amazing secret—and now, at last, he knew it too.

"Of course!" Petula said. "That's why Warren the 2nd drew so many insects. He was studying their movements!"

Warren turned to Mr. Friggs. "But you said the All-Seeing Eye was a weapon."

"I believe it once was," said Mr. Friggs. "A most formidable weapon. It could crush dozens of enemies with a single step."

"And carry villagers to safety," Petula added. "And give soldiers a warm place to sleep. And transport all kinds of supplies."

"Plus the periscope allows you to see for miles in any direction," Warren chimed in. "It truly is an All-Seeing Eye!"

Petula laughed. "And all this time people thought it was some magical trinket. I suppose Annaconda will be very disappointed when she learns the truth."

Warren looked through the periscope and down at the pit. The torrential rains had filled it, making a giant muddy lake, and Annaconda was up to her neck in muck. She was trying to climb up the sides but kept sliding back.

"Helllllp!" she shrieked. "I can't swim!"

Warren called his friends over to look through the peri-scope. "I think we need to save her," he said. "If we don't act now she'll drown."

"Are you crazy?" Petula asked. "After all that she's done?"

Mr. Friggs shook his head. "It's too late, Warren. That pit could turn into a sinkhole at any minute. You'll be sucked down into the center of the earth."

"Hellllllllp!" Annaconda cried again.

"Pleeeease!"

"I can't sit back and do nothing," Warren said. Ignoring Petula's stricken expression, he placed his hand on the panel and powered up the hotel. This time he pushed the lever gently, and the hotel advanced at a more manageable pace, almost tip-toeing to the edge of the pit.

"Not too close," Petula said. "If it collapses, we'll tumble right in!"

"Trust me," Warren said. He was starting to get the hang of the controls—they were sensitive, but he cleared his mind and trusted his instincts, nudging the building ever closer. Then he reached for the cord, pulling the brake and halting its progress.

The hotel trembled and Warren knew he didn't have much time. Rain continued to pelt down and waters were rising; with each passing second the pit widened and deepened. Amid rolling bouts of thunder, Warren could hear Annaconda wailing for help. "If anything happens, Mr. Friggs," Warren said, "just pull the lever toward you and the hotel will walk backward."

Warren pushed the ladder out of the hatch, unfurling it down to the pit far below.

"Are you sure?" Mr. Friggs asked. "It pains me to say this, Warren, but if you were drowning, I don't think Annaconda would save you."

"I'm going to try anyway," Warren said. "Maybe she only married Uncle Rupert to get the All-Seeing Eye, but she's still part of our family. We can't just leave her."

Mr. Friggs nodded. "You're a brave boy. A *good* boy. Your father would be proud."

Warren grabbed the top rung and began descending the ladder.

"Wait!" Petula cried. "Take this! Just in case!"

She reached through the hatch and handed him a perfume bottle. Warren smiled gratefully as he slipped it into his pocket.

"Heeeeeelllp! Pleeeeeaaaase!" Annaconda screamed.

"I'm coming, Auntie!" Warren called back. "Hang on!"

His stomach lurched. He'd always had good reflexes, but maneuvering the twisting ladder was far more challenging than he'd expected.

"Hurrrry!" Annaconda shrieked.

"I'm coming!"

He descended as quickly as possible, practically sliding down the rope. Soon his feet were planted on the bottom rung and his entire body swung perilously over the churning waters. The pit must be thirty feet deep.

"Warrrrren!" Annaconda cried. "Hurry!" She was barely able to stay afloat.

"Grab my hand!" he cried, leaning as far off the ladder as he dared. "I can't get any closer. You'll have to swim to me and I'll pull you out!"

"I can't!" Annaconda's head dipped underwater for one horrifying second. When she broke through the surface, she was slightly closer.

"You're almost there!" Warren cried. "Come on!" After a few seconds of frantic paddling, Annaconda was close enough that her fingernails could graze the tip of Warren's hand. He was straining so hard that he thought his arm might pop out of its socket. "Just...a bit...farther!" he grunted.

Finally he was able to close his hand around her wrist, wincing in pain as her nails dug into his arm. Annaconda proceeded to claw her way up Warren's body as though he were just an extension of the ladder. For someone so thin and bony, she certainly weighed a lot. Her boot heels pressed against his shoulders and she climbed to the upper rungs.

"We did it!" Warren gasped, breathless. He expected Annaconda to look relieved, too. Or happy. Or exhausted.

Instead, she was furious. "You buffoon!" she railed. "Why didn't you tell me the Eye was the hotel?"

"I didn't know!" Warren said.

"I'll never possess the Eye now! Not with you inheriting the hotel on your eighteenth birthday! And after all the work I've done—no! I simply can't allow it!"

With a swift kick of her boot, she knocked Warren off the ladder. He fell backward and hit the water with a splash.

Limbs flailing, he somehow managed to stay afloat, taking in a single choking breath. Through blurred vision he saw that the ground beneath the hotel's pillars was crumbling. The pit was becoming a sink-hole!

Far above, plumes of steam vented from the hotel's smokestacks. With a clanking of horns and a grinding of gears, the building started moving away—without him!

Chapter XVII.

⚓

· IN WHICH ·

WARREN IS DROWNED

(ALMOST)

⚓

ait!" Warren gasped. Despite paddling furiously, he was no match for the roiling waves. He thrashed his legs and struggled to pull himself up, but before long he lost all sense of direction. His lungs burned and his limbs felt like jelly. All his efforts were useless. He sank lower and lower, down to the murky bottom of the pit.

It's over, Warren thought as the inky waters enveloped him. He couldn't hold his breath any longer. The last bit of air bubbled out of his mouth, rising to a surface that seemed impossibly out of reach. In his final moments, Warren remembered the first time his father had brought him up to the roof the hotel, teaching him how to cross the slate tiles without falling. It was one of Warren's earliest memories, and it would also be his last.

Suddenly a dark shape plunged into the water, and something cold and soft wrapped around Warren's waist. The next thing he knew, he was being yanked to the surface. He opened his eyes and saw dozens of fiercely determined pupils staring back at him.

Sketchy! The creature clung to him with two of its tentacles and used the rest to paddle upward. Naturally, Sketchy was an incredibly robust swimmer and even managed to scale the muddy sides of the pit, dragging Warren to safety and depositing him on solid ground.

"Thank you, Sketchy," said Warren, gasping for breath. "I thought I was a goner."

Sketchy raised a tentacle in a salute, then gestured frantically toward the forest. The hotel was walking away! The rope ladder still swung wildly from the building, but there was no sign of Annaconda. Warren guessed that she had climbed to the boiler room and was now controlling the hotel. Surely Mr. Friggs and Petula were no match for her witchery.

"We have to run!" Warren said. He raced after the hotel, slipping and sliding on the muddy ground. Sketchy galloped up alongside, and he hopped onto the creature's back. He urged his friend on, but fallen trees and brambles blocked their way. The hotel was disappearing into the distance. Sketchy sprinted faster—tentacles slithering over the slime—but it was hopeless. The All-Seeing Eye was designed for warfare, and nothing could outrun it. Petula and Friggs were at the mercy of Annaconda.

Just when Warren thought things couldn't get any worse, sharp talons dug into his shoulders. An enormous bird was hoisting him off Sketchy's back. And not just any bird—Isosceles! Sketchy whistled in alarm as the giant vulture hoisted Warren higher and higher, beating her giant wings and soaring above the trees.

"Put me down!" Warren demanded.

"You want to get to the hotel, don't you?" she asked.

Warren was confused. "You're *helping* me?"

"My wretched sister betrayed me," she explained. "She knocked me into the perfumier so she could escape, and I was nearly vacuumed into one of those horrible bottles! I'll never forgive her. Now you and I shall have our revenge!"

With the wind at their backs, Warren and Isosceles soared through the air, moving faster than he ever thought possible. Within minutes they had overtaken the hotel. Isosceles flexed her talons and Warren collapsed onto the old slate roof, the vulture landing alongside him. Thunder cracked overhead and Warren grabbed the old weathervane to steady himself. He knew the roof was the worst place to be in a thunderstorm, but he was glad to be back home.

"Now what?" Warren asked.

"Now we find Annaconda," replied Isosceles.

Suddenly the hotel stopped, and Warren tumbled to the roof's edge, nearly falling over the side. A glint of brass drew his attention: The top of the periscope protruded from the chimney, pivoting left and right. The contraption made a ratcheting sound as it turned to face him.

Warren ran over and peered into the lens. Reflected within its many mirrors were the distorted faces of Petula, Mr. Friggs, and Beatrice. They were shouting frantically but Warren couldn't make out the words.

"What do you see?" Isosceles asked.

"It's my friends!" said Warren. "They're trying to tell me something."

"What are they saying?"

Finally Beatrice removed a card from her deck and held it up to the lens. It was a simple skull and crossbones, the kind you'd see on a pirate flag or a bottle of poison.

"DANGER!"

Warren said. "They're trying to say we're in—"

Warren heard a blood-curdling scream and turned to see Annaconda clambering onto the rooftop. She barreled into Isosceles, knocking her sister onto her back.

"You betrayed me!" Annaconda screamed.

"You betrayed me first!" Isosceles screamed back.

"Let me go, you witch!"

"You're going to pay for what you did! Scalene is trapped in a bottle because of you!"

Isosceles dug her talons into Annaconda's neck and lifted her into the storm, soaring above the hotel. It was hard to see them through the pelting rain—soon they were just tiny shapes in the sky. Warren hoped that Isosceles would carry Annaconda far away and he'd never have to see her again.

But then the horizon flashed with purple light.

Annaconda had used her magic to transform into her spirit animal! Her tiny snail shell slipped through her sister's talons and now she was tumbling down, down, down with the rain. She hit the roof with a *crack!* and bounced across the tiles. With a final bump, she careened off the side of the building, plummeting to the ground.

Warren let out a breath he hadn't realized he was holding. She was gone! He couldn't imagine how anyone, even a snail, could survive such a fall. He crept to the edge of the roof and peered over the side, just to be sure.

A bony hand sprang up at him, clawing at the ledge. The smell of sulfur filled the air and Warren leapt back. Annaconda pulled herself up, her eyes wild and her matted hair plastered to her face. Above them, Isosceles swooped down toward the hotel. "This has gone too far!" she yelled.

Annaconda reached into her dress and pulled out the tooth, now completely covered in carvings. "If I can't have the All-Seeing Eye, *no one can!*" she screamed.

"You're out of spells!" Warren cried. "There's nothing you can do!"

"Oh, but I can!" Annaconda hissed.

"No!" Isosceles shrieked. She hovered over the roof, beating her giant wings. "The tooth can't handle any more! If you carve over all those old spells, you'll destroy us all!"

"Exactly!" Annaconda shrieked. "I'm going to destroy this hotel and everyone in it!"

She began chanting words that Warren didn't recognize, causing the carvings on the tooth to glow with a supernatural light.

Isosceles gave Warren a pitying look. "Sorry, kid. I tried. It's too late now—you're all doomed!" And with that she took off like a bullet, disappearing into the storm clouds.

Annaconda continued chanting in a strange guttural language; as she did so, new carvings lashed the tooth like cracks across an icy pond. A jagged bolt of lightning struck the hotel, but Annaconda didn't even notice. Electricity lifted her hair, causing strands to writhe around her face like snakes.

The tooth glowed brighter, and Warren felt the hotel shaking beneath him. A tearing sound ripped through the air as if the sky was being split in two. Annaconda raised the tooth over her head as lighting bolts zapped it with more dark energy than it could handle. She let out a long, terrible scream and her eyes shone white.

The force of the tooth's blast was so intense, so blinding, that Warren almost forgot to grab the bottle tucked inside his jacket. He thought he might be too late, but he pulled the cork and a blast of cool air escaped; he could see the crackling halo of poisoned light leave the tooth and rush toward him. Terrified, he nearly dropped the bottle but somehow managed to hold on. The glass burned a molten orange and grew painfully hot, but he would not let go.

"Noooooo!" Annaconda shrieked. She tried to run but there was nowhere left to go—she had reached the edge of the roof. Warren watched with horror and fascination as Annaconda's features stretched and melted until she looked like a smear of paint. She was sucked into the bottle with a loud *SCHWOOOOOOP!*, the tooth clattering uselessly to the ground.

Warren popped the cork into the bottle and then peered through the glass. He half

expected to see a miniature Annaconda looking back, but all he could make out was a swirl of cloudy magic.

"Over here!" Warren turned to see Petula calling to him. She was leaning out his attic window and waving. Warren picked up the tooth and ran to join her. Beatrice was there, too; she extended both arms and helped Warren navigate the slippery surface, gently lowering him through the window. He was never so relieved to be back in his tiny room.

"We hurried as fast as we could!" Petula cried. "Where's Annaconda?"

"Right here," Warren said, handing the bottle to Beatrice. She inspected it carefully, then slipped it inside her robe and patted Warren on the head. With another *fwip!* she presented a card depicting a trophy. He blushed with pride.

"You did it!" Petula cried. "Mr. Friggs was so worried, but I knew you could do it!"

"Where is Mr. Friggs? Is he okay?"

"He's back in the control room. I would make a portal to get us there, but my arm is useless. Let's hurry and tell him the good news!"

As they made their way down the stairs, they noticed that the sleeping guests scattered throughout the halls were beginning to stir.

"Annaconda's spell must have broken when you captured her," Petula said. A few of the guests seemed disgruntled, but many were merely confused. There was no mention of treasure, no talk of the All-Seeing Eye. In fact, most were unsure why they had come to such a dilapidated hotel in the first place.

The barbarian grabbed Warren by the lapels. "Where am I?" he asked. "Who captured me and brought me to this dreary place?"

"You're free to check out if you like, sir," Warren said. "I'm heading to the lobby right now."

In the lobby, Warren found Uncle Rupert stumbling in circles, looking as if he'd just awakened from a deep nap. "What's going on?" he asked. "Why are the guests sleeping on the floor?"

"It's a long story," Warren said. He realized he would have to tell his uncle the truth about Aunt Annaconda. "I have some bad news and I'm not quite sure how to tell you."

"Out with it, boy! What's the trouble?"

"Well . . . Aunt Annaconda is gone."

Rupert blinked in confusion. "Who?"

"Annaconda. Your wife."

"My wife?" Rupert laughed, and his stomach jiggled merrily. "What are you going on about, boy? I don't have a wife!"

Petula pulled Warren aside and whispered in his ear: "That was no ordinary sleep spell! Annaconda must have supplemented it with a memory wipe. She wanted to be extra certain that no one would ever find the Eye!"

"Look at all these guests," Rupert exclaimed, studying the lobby in wonderment. "Where did they come from? What are they doing here?"

There was so much to say, Warren didn't even know where to begin. In time he would explain everything to his uncle, but for now, it was best to leave it be.

The front doors opened with a crash and Sketchy charged inside, dripping wet.

The creature flung its tentacles around Warren, pulling him into a giant hug. Rupert screamed and ran out of the lobby, convinced that his nephew had just been devoured.

"Thank you for rescuing me," Warren said, patting the monster's head. "Because of your help, I was able to stop Aunt Anna-conda. She's never going to bother us again."

Sketchy whistled happily and wiggled around like a hula dancer. The guests stopped grumbling to admire the perfor-mance. It was really quite beautiful, and at the end of the dance the onlookers offered a polite round of applause. Warren was enjoying it so much, he almost didn't see Mr. Friggs hobbling toward him.

"Warren, my boy!" Mr. Friggs cried with relief. "I thought we were doomed, but you've saved us!"

"I couldn't have done it without all of you," Warren said, turning to Petula and

Beatrice. "I know the hotel is bizarre and it's a bit run-down and there's a lot I need to learn about the All-Seeing Eye, but I love it here and I never want to leave."

"And now you don't have to," Mr. Friggs said with a wink. "You can see the whole world without ever leaving the comforts of home!"

They walked to the nearest window and looked outside. The storm had finally passed and the clouds parted to reveal a brilliant sun. The hotel had come to rest on a small hill overlooking miles and miles of countryside. Off on the horizon, Warren could see the towers and smokestacks of a distant city.

"The only question left is," Petula said,

"WHERE DO YOU WANT TO GO FIRST?"

EPILOGUE

From the top of a step ladder, Rupert adjusted the wooden sign that hung over the hotel entrance. "Is that good?" he asked.

Warren tilted his head. "Just a little to right! No, your other right! That's it!"

With a loud *BANG! BANG! BANG!* Rupert nailed the sign in place:

=⊨ The ⊨=

WARREN

THE WORLD'S FIRST AND ONLY

TRAVELING HOTEL!

GRAND RE-OPENING!

Underneath was a smaller sign that said "Vacancy," but Warren knew it wouldn't be vacant much longer. They had opened for business just two days ago and already the hotel was drawing attention. Everywhere they went the local newspapers wrote about the extraordinary mechanical marvel. Warren's favorite headline was: "This Roadhouse Is on the Road! Catch Your Zzzs Here . . . If You Can Keep Up!"

A seagull squawked overhead as it soared on the wind, and Warren turned to admire the view. On this morning, the hotel was parked at the edge of a rocky beach. The ocean looked far grander than it ever had in his imagination—he loved the way the light and shadows danced across its surface. He had sketched it a dozen times and couldn't wait to draw it again. Now that the hotel

was fully staffed, he had plenty of time for his artistic pursuits.

"Warren!" Petula shouted. He looked up and saw his friend standing on the roof, cleaning the periscope lens. "Mom's fingers are tingling, so that storm will probably be here soon. We should be on our way!"

"Roger that!" Warren called back. Since becoming the captain of a moving hotel, he was using words he learned from a book Mr. Friggs had given him called *The Vernacular of Pilots, Drivers, Captains, and Ploughmen, Etcetera*. It made his commands and directions seem much more official.

Warren faced the ocean and waved his arms. "Ahoy there, Sketchy! Come ashore! We're getting ready for departure!"

His monstrous friend crested the waves and waggled its tentacles happily. Then the monster bounded onto the beach and shook itself off, spraying droplets in all directions.

"I'll race you!" Warren cried, and Sketchy leapt past him, landing on the porch with time to spare.

"Don't let that thing track sand inside!" Rupert warned as he hopped off the ladder. "I just polished the floors!"

"Sketchy's not a *thing*, Uncle Rupert! It's a friend!"

Sketchy paused to stick out its tongue, making Rupert cringe. He was still terrified of the creature, and the sight of its purple tongue only increased his discomfort.

Inside, the hotel lobby looked better than ever. The wallpaper had been scrubbed and the marble floors sparkled. Warren and his friends had spent days preparing for life on the go. That meant bolting all the furniture down, strapping books into bookcases, adding extra nails to paintings, and building cabinets to store the many fragile antiques. It was a lot of work but everyone helped—even Uncle Rupert. Once Mr. Friggs explained that only a Warren could control the hotel's movements, Rupert decided that his nephew deserved full management duties. From now on, Warren the 13th would supervise everything, though of course Rupert would continue to offer advice, between naps.

Warren and Sketchy headed downstairs, where Chef Bunion was busy preparing lunch. "We're heading out in a few minutes," Warren said. "Secure the cookware."

"Aye, aye, Captain!" Chef replied. "Can my junior cook lend a few hands?"

Sketchy's many tentacles were handy around the kitchen, and the creature had quickly established itself as Chef's most trusted helper. The monster could strap pots and pans to the racks and latch the cabinets in half the time it would take Chef to do it on his own. Sketchy was rewarded with an extra-large pudding cookie; it whistled happily and gobbled up the treat.

Warren left Sketchy to enjoy his snack and then made his way to the control room, easing himself into the pilot seat. Rupert followed along and dropped into a hammock strung from one wall to the other. Whenever the hotel was in motion, he enjoyed swaying while sipping fruity drinks.

Warren pressed the intercom and announced, "Prepare for departure!"

Petula responded from her perch on the roof. "All clear!"

Warren placed his palm on the control panel, activating the machinery. The hotel rumbled to life amid the clanks of cogs and hisses of steam. Using books from Mr. Friggs's library, Warren had identified and labeled most of the buttons and levers, and now he steered the vessel with confidence.

As the hotel rose on its mighty arachnid

legs, Warren flicked the tooth, which he hung on a string above the controls as a sort of good luck charm. Then he typed in the activation code and gently pressed forward on the thrust. The hotel walked away from the ocean with a loud *CLANG! CLANG! CLANG!* Nearby beach dwellers peered out their cottage windows, gaping at the enormous building lumbering across the land. For as large and as awkward as it was, the hotel took precise steps, avoiding structures and people as it marched toward the countryside.

Children and dogs emerged from their homes to chase after it, hollering and barking with glee; Petula waved from the rooftop as the hotel departed. The six ravens from the chimney circled over her head, then settled into a new birdhouse that she and Mr. Friggs had constructed especially for them. The birds squawked a happy tune as the hotel clomped along.

Beatrice had taken over the eighth-floor room that used to belong to Annaconda's sisters. She sat down in a comfortable overstuffed armchair and then reached down for her violin. The ravens were squawking just beyond her window, and she decided to accompany them with her instrument. It was time to take a break from the witch hunting. She plucked the strings gracefully and gazed out at the passing scenery.

In the library, Mr. Friggs looked up from a wall map. He had placed a pin over the rocky beach they just left. Where would they go next? It was anybody's guess. For years, he'd assumed that his adventuring days were behind him—but now, thanks to Warren, he'd once again see new places.

Down in the Hall of Ancestors, the portraits of Warren's forefathers swayed on their hooks. As Warren gazed at them now, he certainly thought they all looked pleased, especially Warren the 12th. The All-Seeing Eye was no longer a secret or a weapon. Instead it was being used to bring rest, relaxation, and quality hospitality to people all over the world.

A new portrait now graced the walls of the Hall of Ancestors—it was a bit larger than the others, to squeeze everyone in. With confident strokes of smoky charcoal, the artist had drawn the smiling faces of Rupert, Petula, Beatrice, Mr. Friggs, Chef Bunion, and Sketchy—his whole happy family—gathered around him,